Dear Reader,

The book you are holding came about in a rather different way to most others. It was funded directly by readers through a new website: Unbound. Unbound is the creation of three writers. We started the company because we believed there had to be a better deal for both writers and readers. On the Unbound website, authors share the ideas for the books they want to write directly with readers. If enough of you support the book by pledging for it in advance, we produce a beautifully bound special subscribers' edition and distribute a regular edition and ebook wherever books are sold, in shops and online.

This new way of publishing is actually a very old idea (Samuel Johnson funded his dictionary this way). We're just using the internet to build each writer a network of patrons. At the back of this book, you'll find the names of all the people who made it happen.

Publishing in this way means readers are no longer just passive consumers of the books they buy, and authors are free to write the books they really want. They get a much fairer return too – half the profits their books generate, rather than a tiny percentage of the cover price.

If you're not yet a subscriber, we hope that you'll want to join our publishing revolution and have your name listed in one of our books in the future. To get you started, here is a £5 discount on your first pledge. Just visit unbound.com, make your pledge and type **johnny5** in the promo code box when you check out.

Thank you for your support,

Dan, Justin and John
Founders, Unbound

JOHNNY
RUIN

JOHNNY RUIN

DAN DALTON

Unbound

This edition first published in 2018

Unbound
6th Floor Mutual House, 70 Conduit Street, London W1S 2GF
www.unbound.com

© Dan Dalton, 2018

Quote from *The Cocktail Party* © T. S. Eliot, *The Complete Poems and Plays of T. S. Eliot*
reprinted by permission of Faber and Faber Ltd.

Text Design by PDQ

A CIP record for this book is available from the British Library

ISBN 978-1-78352-505-8 (trade hbk)
ISBN 978-1-78352-506-5 (ebook)
ISBN 978-1-78352-504-1 (limited edition)

Printed in Great Britain by Clays Ltd, St Ives Plc

1 3 5 7 9 8 6 4 2

MIX
Paper from
responsible sources
FSC
www.fsc.org
FSC® C018179

For Rob

What is hell? Hell is oneself.
Hell is alone, the other figures in it
Merely projections. There is nothing to
escape from
And nothing to escape to. One is always alone.

T. S. Eliot, *The Cocktail Party*

One
California / Dreaming

Start with the weather. Cool, calm, twenty-two degrees. Not so much weather as an absence of it. Above, the ceiling of trees breaks to reveal a solitary cloud. Then a second, floating towards the first. If you can only see one cloud, you're not looking at enough sky.

He calls down to me, asks what I'm doing. I tell him I'm writing a book. A beam of light falls across his face. He rocks back on his heels, squints. *What's it about*, he says. I try not to stare, to mumble. *Grief*, I say. We sit, surrounded by giant redwoods. Sun filters through a canopy of leaves. The Japanese have a word for that. I'm not Japanese. Neither is he. He draws a breath, asks who died. *I did*, I say. He shakes his head. *Tough break*, he says. He means it.

The first thing you learn about Jon Bon Jovi is that he's very sincere.

I'm ten, riding my bike through the woods, all oak and pine and silver birch. I choose a tree with low branches, climb all the way to the top. From there I can see the whole valley. I stay for hours. When I finally get home, it's dark out. Mum is angry, shouting. *Where have you been.* I blame the tree.

The sequoia is native to California, and California is a long way from London. Jon sits atop a fallen trunk as high as a house. He might be meditating. He might be hung-over. *This is the forest of the mind,* he says. He doesn't open his eyes. *Oh,* I say. *That clears it right up.*

The first time I kiss her I never want to stop.

My first Bon Jovi record was *Cross Road*. 1994. I wore out the cassette. Jon circa *Cross Road* had the shorter hair, the Henley shirt, the John Lennon sunglasses. Gone was the poodle perm, the floor-length leather coat. 1994 Jon Bon Jovi was the coolest man I'd ever seen. This is that Jon Bon Jovi. The same one who's urinating off the top of the tree trunk, his stream of hot piss narrowly missing me. He shouts down. *Look out below.* It's too late.

The second thing you learn about Jon Bon Jovi is that he isn't shy.

I've been in this forest once before. The one with all the redwoods. A long time ago. But this isn't just that forest. There's oak, pine, silver birch. All the forests I've known scattered in and among. All my selves. There I am, eleven years old, building a treehouse. There I am, at fifteen, getting a hand job against a tree from a girl I met on holiday. I'm too worried about ants to come. There I am at twenty-seven, walking with my future ex-wife. Here I am, thirty-two, sitting in a forest, surrounded by the flickering ghosts of my past selves. Ghosts are just echoes you can see. I write that down.

I get any piss on you, Jon says, thrusting his hips so his dick spins like a helicopter.

The first time I kiss her I never want to stop. I know she's going to break my heart.

Set the scene. It's a crisp autumn afternoon in a Californian forest and I have no idea how I got here. Her name is on the breeze blowing through the leaves. The sun casts long shadows of the redwoods around me, trunks as wide as thirty feet ascending far into the sky. Dust and debris float through sunbeams, catching the light like airborne glitter, rising into the canopy above. It's heaven on earth. Except it can't be earth, and I don't believe in heaven. I'm pretty sure I'm dead.

You're not dead, Jon says. He sits next to me, chewing a blade of grass he plucked from the undergrowth. Hopefully not the undergrowth he just pissed on. Piss or no, he exists with the kind of effortless cool you can't help but envy. He speaks without looking up. *What do you remember.*

Her lips were so soft I gasped the first time I kissed her. I was hard the second we touched. Later, just her scent would get me hard. Before I touched her, before I tasted her. Now all it takes is the thought of her. Now all I have are memories.

Somewhere in the forest I'm eighteen, falling in love for the first time. Somewhere in the forest she's not returning the sentiment. She already has a boyfriend, isn't in the market for another.

Somewhere in the forest I'm missing the wood for the trees.

I say: *Ketamine.*
He says: *Ketamine what.*
I say: *That's what I remember.*

He says: *Why would you take Ketamine.*
I say: *I don't know. I was tired. I wasn't thinking.*
He says: *Well you know what they say. Hindsight is sixty-forty.*

That thing you read about Ketamine curing depression. A study showed a single transfusion can lift your mood. Permanently. Plus you get a pretty great high. You can't get the treatment in the UK. Not yet. But you can get Ketamine. Dose yourself with small amounts. And I did.

I'm ten, riding my bike through a forest. Oak, pine, silver birch. I choose one with low branches, climb all the way to the top. I can see across the tops of trees for miles around. Distant villages, church spires, rivers, smoke. I can hear birds, watch clouds. I stay for hours, only leaving when it's too dark to see. Mum is angry. She asks where I've been. I blame the night. It came too early.

The truth is I didn't know how to get down.

We've been silent a moment. Jon turns to me. *Have you figured it out yet.* I ask if I'm dreaming. *Not exactly,* he says. Her voice on the wind now, purring. *You make me feel so good.* I shut my eyes. The wind is only a light breeze. Still it stings.

Shit, Jon says. *Slow to catch on, aren't we.* He casts his hands up, conducting the wind. *We're in your head, champ. Your mind. Your memories. Your imagination. All this is you.*

It feels like we're being watched. The forest shifts in front of me. In the tree line ahead, a shape moves between branches, it's face and form unfixed, a memory I can't place. I ask Jon if he sees it too, but by the time the words arrive it's already gone.

I'm twenty-two, walking among redwoods, taking pictures on a disposable camera. Three weeks later I'll get the prints back to find them washed out, blotchy. Too much sun.

Here, now, the light turns harsh, stabs through the trees. I look at Jon, spots of colour burned into my retina. I ask if I'm doing this. He stands, dusts himself off. *Too much time in your head is a terrible thing*, he says. I tell him we've only been here an hour. *You've been here your whole life, chief*, he says. He takes my hand, pulls me to my feet. *I should know, I've been here with you.*

I was born in 1983. The year John Bongiovi changed his name to Jon Bon Jovi, had his first hit with the band he named after himself. His manager, Doc McGhee, suggested the change, the band name. Bon Jovi was easier to remember, to spell. Plus, it worked for Van Halen.

My first name never fit right. Always felt too formal. I was given others, nicknames. Nothing stuck. As a kid I used to try on names for fun. Later I used pseudonyms for writing. I wanted to seem cooler, more likeable. Plus I couldn't use mine. Not any more. After her my name was ruin.

Jon is carving his name into the trunk of the redwood. *Didn't you already piss on it*, I say. He finishes, folds his knife, blows away the dust. *Piss fades*, he says. *Names last for ever.*

I stand at the base of a tree, look up. The whole thing feels like it's falling. A trick of the mind. *We can stay*, Jon says. *Enjoy the sunset. Or we go. There's a road just past the edge of the forest.* I look at the sun, there's still plenty of light left. *If we go*, I say, *will I wake up.* Jon puts his hand to my forehead, the way a parent might. *No promises*, he says. *But it beats sitting here waiting.*

I wonder what would happen if one of the redwoods fell. Not my best idea. We barely manage to roll out of the way as the one in front of us topples to the ground. It takes out half a dozen others on its way, the ground rising, breaking open as roots are torn from the earth. Maybe this is a trick of the mind, too. Maybe everything here is. *I guess we go, then,* I say.

The first time I kiss her I never want to stop. Nothing lasts for ever.

I'm thirty-two, riding my bike through the forest with Jon Bon Jovi. We peddle hard, like every kid in an eighties' movie. Redwoods fall. Creaking, cracking, crashing. Splinters the size of small cars shoot past. Roots rise up like walls. The forest of my mind is collapsing. I'm folding in on myself.

If a tree falls in a forest and Jon Bon Jovi is with you when it happens, is it still a figment of your imagination.

What do you remember, he says. The ground below us shakes, crumbles away. *I told you,* I say. We launch off upended roots, flying downhill, ducking between trunks, under branches. *I didn't ask what you took,* he says. I'm quiet a moment. Working up the nerve to tell him. *I tried to kill myself,* I say. It comes out louder than I'd intended. *I know, buddy,* he says, swerving to avoid a tree. *You do,* I say. He nods. *Yeah, I do.* He looks so very cool on a BMX.

The edge of the forest is in sight. He's slightly ahead of me, shouting. *Your book. The one about grief. You should save that reveal, the whole suicide thing, for the end of the second act.*

Something most people don't know about Jon is that he's really pretty great at narrative critique.

Something most people don't know about me is I've never seen giant redwoods.

But I always say I have.

Two

Nevada / Unremembered

We're half a tank of gas past the edge of the desert when the drugs kick in. Somewhere beyond the boundaries of this endless expanse my body is metabolising the Ketamine. The effect is hallucinatory. The bright burn of the sunrise ahead an explosion of dancing flame, a hellfire scorching the night itself. It melts the moon from the sky, a waterfall of dust collecting on the desert floor. We're driving straight towards the fire. I step on the gas.

I'm eight or nine walking to school, playing a game where I name every car that drives past: Ford Fiesta. Ford Escort. Ford Sierra. Just about everyone has a Ford. When I don't know one, I turn around, read the badge. Some days I get all the way there without missing one.

My day job is I write tweets for a brand. JoeSeal. It's a wood stain. You know, *For the regular Joe*. What I do with JoeSeal is I tweet vaguely philosophical statements about life from the perspective of a tin of wood stain. I want to write novels, but this is what pays the bills.

Sample tweet: *You can't protect your heart but you can protect your fence. Buy JoeSeal.*

I ask Jon if Bukowski would have written tweets for a brand. *You're overthinking this,* he says.

I've been driving through the night. We swapped the bikes for a Cadillac. A big boat of a car. The kind people are always driving in books and films. We've covered countless miles of blacktop, air whipping over the windscreen, damping the smell of hot rubber, gasoline.

I yawn, feel the tired ache of unstretched legs. The plains are so vast it feels like we're surfing the horizon, ploughing along our asphalt furrow down orange strands of light. The sun is rising, turning the world a thousand colours at once, all of them golden. I'm wide awake. It's morning.

There's nothing for miles around, but there are billboards. Freestanding scaffolds angled to the road, selling me memories I'd rather forget. A stupid thing I said once in a muscular font, thirty feet high. A little further down the road, a billboard with her face. In the caption she's saying she loves me. Thirty seconds later on another billboard she's telling me she can't do this any more.

Establish the quest. For a while I was flying above the car, watching myself drive it, but by the time Jon wakes up the sun is halfway to the top of the sky and my body has come back down. *Want me to drive,* he says. I ask him where we're going. He grins. *We're already there.*

It's not so much a destination as a journey.
And what the fuck does that mean, I say.
It means shut up and enjoy this part.

A passing billboard tells me I'm no fun.

In JoeSeal parlance, a Joe can be a woman too, but only because people complained. Right before I started they did a limited edition JaneSeal for International Women's Day. The tin was pink. It was a total PR disaster. But sales of JoeSeal went up by 34 per cent.

Sample tweet: *Be the fence you wish to see in the world. Buy JoeSeal.*

Think of the mind as a map, Jon says. *You have places for different things. Memories, thoughts, feelings. You get my drift.* I look at the ocean of desert touching the sky in every direction. I ask him what I store here. He looks around. *Not much, I'd wager.*

The trick is most people are bored. Horribly so. Most everything people do is motivated by that. Bored being single, get a girlfriend, bored of that, get married. Have a kid, have an affair, get a divorce, buy something expensive, fast. Work, work, work. Drink. Fuck. Sleep. My grandparents lived into their nineties. I guess what I'm saying is I don't want another sixty years of being bored.

I say: *Are those bats.*
He says: *Definitely not.*

People say talking to yourself is the first sign of madness, but I don't agree. Talking to yourself is just practising for conversations you haven't had yet. The first sign of madness is not realising the person you're speaking to is you.

I waste the hours by naming the cars passing on the other side of the highway. It's pretty easy. After a while I realise I'm a passenger in those cars too. They're all cars I've owned.

My first car was a 1992 Ford Fiesta. I got it in 2004 for £100. It was held together by rust and hope, red paint faded pink. I named him Steve McQueen, because he was so cool. He fell apart eventually, more holes than things holding him together. But he was fun, for a while.

Sample tweet: *Delay the inevitable. Buy JoeSeal.*

Think of it this way, Jon says. *This is the Land of Left Behind. People, places, things that you once knew. Friends you forgot. Lovers you never loved. You know.* I mention his solo album. He laughs. Another thing you learn about Jon Bon Jovi is that it's pretty hard to hurt his feelings. On account of him being a projection of your subconscious and all.

The hair. That smile. It's easy to forget that this isn't Jon Bon Jovi. Not really. More like Non Jovi. A character I've conjured, plucked from the back of an album cover. And yet I'm happy to forget. To pretend. To feel like a kid again, in the company of the coolest man I've ever seen.

In 1990, Jon took a road trip on his motorcycle. After four hit albums and back-to-back world tours he was beaten, worn down, burned out. He put the band on blocks, stepped away a while. He cut his hair, rode between small towns, worked on songs that would become *Keep the Faith.*

Then he wrote the soundtrack for *Young Guns II.* Most people forget that was a solo project. He won the Golden Globe, but Sondheim beat him to the Oscar. It didn't matter. He'd found what he was looking for. In the desert, he cast off the old and remade himself anew.

In this desert, he's standing in his seat, pointing at a billboard advertising an unflattering picture I accidentally took of myself on my phone. *Oh, buddy... how many chins is that.*

She said she loved my body, kissed every inch of me to prove it. I can still feel her lips on my skin. Her soft, soft lips. The ones that remade me anew.

We drive past Steve McQueen, more rust than car, lying desolate where I parked him, at the side of the road in my mind, somewhere along the highway in the Land of Lost Things.

Maybe I should put the band on hiatus.
But you're not in a band, Jon says.
It was a figure of speech, I say.
You're a figure of speech.

In 2005, I took a road trip across the US. I drove 10,000 miles, hit thirty states in thirty days. Most of it looked like this. Miles of nothing, then endless suburbs littered with strip malls and chain restaurants. You can drive anywhere in America and find yourself exactly where you started, on a six-lane highway between a Sizzler and an Outback Steakhouse.

Sample tweet: *Home is where the fence is. Buy JoeSeal.*

Billboard: *Kill yourself.*

Another car I had was a 1985 Mitsubishi 4x4 named Magnum PI, on account of the bull bars looking like a moustache. The front seats had independent suspension, which you're meant to use for off-road driving, but I used for car sex. A girlfriend and I would spend nights driving to quiet spots so she could straddle me while we rode around, let the seat do the work for us.

We drive past the scene on the opposite side of the road, her face contorted, mine straining to watch the road as the seat rocks us towards ecstasy. As the 4x4 fades in the rear view, Jon punches my arm, congratulates me on sex I had a decade ago.

Somewhere out in the plains, I see a boy, laughing, riding his bike. Behind him, another boy doing the same. My brother and me. We must be eleven, twelve. We're happy. *I guess I've lost a lot,* I say.

An old friend stands at the side of the road, thumb raised, trying to hitch a ride. Paul. I don't stop. Paul and I haven't talked in a long time, and the reason we haven't talked is I'm kinda embarrassed about the way my life has gone. I don't want him to see me like this.

Jon is standing up in the passenger seat, arms out like this boat of a car is the goddamn *Titanic.* He's grinning, trying, failing to shout things into rushing air. I ask him what he's doing. *Living,* he says, and I tell him none of this is real. He grins. *I'm just making the best with what I have.*

On a passing billboard we're forty feet high and happy.

I guess what I'm saying is I don't want another sixty years of being alone.

You can be too happy, I say, to Jon, to no one in particular. *Horse shit,* he says. *Look at dogs. Dogs are just about as happy as you can be.* I shake my head, ask if he's heard of Happy Tail. *It's where a dog wags his tail so hard against something that it splits at the tip and bleeds,* I say. *They end up spraying blood everywhere.* We drive in silence a moment. *You can be too happy.*

Jon says: *You have a unique talent for ruining everything.*
Jon says: *Pick the guy up, I'll drive.*

We switch seats. Jon spins us around, sailing the car on to the dirt, back across both lanes. Dusk falls, the sky glowing orange where it meets the desert. High above, light blue gives way to black. I look up and realise that the stars are just scratches. The night is worn, faded like an old photograph, processed through filters that replicate analogue wear.

How long will this take.
You mean picking him up.
This whole thing. This journey.
How long can you go without water.
Depends, I say. *Five days. A week maybe.*
Then we should probably try and finish before that.

I take out my notebook, start writing. Jon reads over my shoulder. *That really how you're going to start.* I cover my notes with my hand. He pushes a cassette into the stereo. Brian Eno. It doesn't fit the scene. It's utterly perfect. *Hey,* he says. *It's your story.*

He puts his foot on the dash, taps a beat on his thigh with the flat of his palm. He smiles. It's a smile that's sold a million albums. Here, now, among forgotten memories and discarded lives, I realise I haven't listened to a Bon Jovi record in a decade.

Sample tweet: *You won't be alive to see it fade. Buy JoeSeal.*

Three

Nevada / Unremembered, Part II

We crossed into darkness without realising. The night is subtle like that, draping slowly then all at once. It's cool out, not cold. We keep the top down. Jon wouldn't have it any other way. He has one leg hanging over the door, his bare foot resting on the wing mirror, driving at 88 miles an hour exactly. I know this because he made a point of telling me. He has a single finger at the bottom of the steering wheel, tapping his free hand on his thigh, keeping time with a beat I can't hear. It's been half an hour since we picked up our hitcher. We still haven't said a word.

I'm twenty-two. My best friend Paul and I are sneaking out of Los Angeles before daylight brings gridlock. We plan to hit thirty states in thirty days, drive more than 10,000 miles. It'll be the trip of a lifetime.

Here, now, in the back seat of the Cadillac, Paul sits quietly, riding bitch with the friend who left him behind and his rock-star valet. He leans forward. *Are you really Bon Jovi.* Jon nods. *Mate, I love that song you did. What's it called, 'Sweet Child o' Mine'. Absolute tune, that one.* Jon grips the steering wheel tight, mutters, *Thanks.* I don't try to hide my smirk.

I don't remember my first car crash. Mum told me the story. We were stopped at a red light when someone hit us from behind. My bottom teeth went through my lower lip. I still have the scar. It's like a diary entry someone wrote for me, a souvenir of something I don't recall.

I'm twenty-two, on my road trip with Paul, drinking stubbies in a Motel 6. He's drunk, screaming at the top of his lungs. *What's in the box! What's in the box!* I have to punch him in the face to get him to go to sleep. He'll wake up in a few hours with an aching jaw and I'll tell him he fell over.

Jon taps the brakes twice, swings the steering wheel so the car swerves in the lane. I wake from a half sleep. *What the fuck.* He laughs, tells me the car is dancing. Mum used to do this, when I was a kid. It was hilarious then. *You don't have any fucking music on,* I say. He brakes in time with his beat. *No, champ,* he says. *You don't have any fucking music on.*

I turn around, kneel in my seat. Paul looks up. *Remember those sisters we picked up at that karaoke bar,* he says. *Took a bullet for you that night, pal. Yours was all right, mind.* I wince at his words. There's a pause that carries too long. I try changing the subject.

Where is it you're off to.
Oh, you know. Here, there.
This is the middle of nowhere.
Remember that dancer I fucked.
Where is it you need to get to, I say.
Great legs. Why didn't I see her again.
Maybe the girlfriend you were living with.
Oh, true, he says. *Shame though. Great legs.*

The exchange is a little unfair. These are his words, but they don't represent him, all of him. And yet they're the reason he's here, in the back of my mind. We haven't spoken in years.

Perhaps because he reminds me of a me I'd rather forget. Perhaps he reminds me of someone I still am.

Jon speaks. *It's Paul, right.* Paul nods. *You two used to be buddies,* Jon says. *So why don't you talk any more.* I already know the answer. Jon should too. The night is crisp and my breath fogs a little. But I'm not cold. It's never cold here. *Honestly,* Paul says, *it gets a bit boring after a while.*

The first car hits us from behind. Shunts us forward. There's confusion, the cry of torn metal. Tyres screech. We're hit again from the side. A different car. *What the fuck is—* Jon starts. He doesn't get to finish. Another shunt pushes us out of our lane, into oncoming traffic. Jon swerves us back into the right lane, straight into a broadside from a four-wheel drive. Jon speeds up, goes on the offensive, but one of them hits our rear right side. The back of the car swings out. Jon fights the wheel as we spin across the lane divider. The car is dancing, but not to our beat.

We come to a stop. I start to ask if everyone is okay when a speeding truck slams into us. The car rolls in slow motion. The ground hits me hard. I'm not sure how long I'm out. When I open my eyes, I'm lying in the dirt at the side of the road. Jon is nearby. Then I see Paul.

The last time I saw Paul he nearly killed us both in a car crash. That was a decade ago. Now he's a mangled body in a wrecked car in my mind. The night drapes slowly and then all at once.

Sample tweet: *You can't protect everything. Buy JoeSeal.*

Jon stands up, dusts himself off. He walks over to where I'm standing. *Shit. Some ride.* I look down at Paul's body. *Tell that to Paul.* Jon asks if he's dead. *Either that or he's really fucking unwell,* I say. Jon leans close, puts his arm around my shoulder. *You lose some, you lose some.*

I brush his hand away. *What good are you,* I say. *You act like you know everything. You don't know shit.* The road is littered with metal and glass and Paul. *I know all kinds of things,* Jon says. *I know it's pretty difficult to kill yourself with Ketamine.*

He starts walking. I watch Paul turn to dust and bones, his remains carried away by the wind. Jon puts a hand up to stop his hat going with them. *You coming,* he says. The coolest man I've never met walks from highway into shadow. I pick up my notebook, follow along behind.

On our road trip around the US I fell asleep at the wheel. I'd been driving all night. Paul was asleep in the passenger seat. It was only a second. Maybe less. A microsleep, they call it. Long enough that I woke up too close to the Jeep in front, had to swerve to avoid hitting it. The driver of the Jeep honked her horn, shouted inaudible insults into my rear view. I pulled over soon after. Paul slept through the whole thing. I never told him.

I'm thirty-one. It's our first road trip together. She's spent the first hour telling me about all the horrific car accidents she's seen. Decapitations. Drivers who'd killed their entire families after falling asleep at the wheel. A car crushed when a large container fell from a lorry, squashed so flat it was almost impossible to salvage the remains of the driver, passenger and two children. *Looked like a panini,* she says. She asks if I want to talk about something else. *I don't mind,* I say, picturing a panini leaking people juice.

Jon says: *Wanna get a move on there.*
I say: *I haven't written today.*
He says: *Write tomorrow.*
I say: *Bukowski wrote every day.*
He says: *You've never read Bukowski.*

At the side of the highway up ahead there's a giant anatomically correct neon heart. It must be fifty feet high, flickering back and forth between whole and broken. You see things like this out in the desert. Huge concrete dinosaurs. World's Biggest Thermometer. World's Biggest Broken Heart.

The night Paul died he was driving too fast, racing over a quiet stretch of highway in the black of night. When I asked him to slow down, he took off his seat belt, sped up. *I'm not going to—* he started. He didn't get to finish. We hit a car stopped in our lane. He went through the windshield, bounced off the back of the car we hit, landed in several different places on the road. The other car was empty. The driver had left his hazard warning lights on, walked to find a phone.

When they find me I'm trying to account for all his pieces. *I can't find his face,* I say, pointing at the rest of his head. Later the police would tell me there wasn't a face to find. He'd hit the road with enough speed that he slid along the tarmac for thirty, forty feet, shredding his clothes, obliterating his face. It had ground off as he slid, asphalt like sandpaper on soft flesh, a red skid mark in his wake. I'd stood in the remnants, trying to collect his teeth, not realising the jaw that once held them no longer existed. The coroner will say his neck broke passing through the windshield. A small mercy. There will be a closed casket at the funeral.

Sample tweet: *Live fast, die young, leave a good-looking fence. Buy JoeSeal.*

Above us, stars shoot in slow motion and I wonder if a star shooting in slow motion is just a star. We've been walking for what feels like hours. Jon turns to me. *What do you want most,* he says. *Right now.* I see her face, her hair, her eyes rolling back as she comes. *I want to go home.* He doesn't reply. I can't tell if he's nodding or bobbing his head to some internal rhythm. Musicians. I walk with my eyes on my feet, nearly don't notice when Jon stops, looks up. I follow his gaze to a house in the distance. *Wonder if anybody's home,* he says, but I know he knows the answer.

In the distance, a neon sign flickers in the dark, four red and blue words burn against the black of night behind them: *You are not here.*

As I watch, the third word flickers and falls dark, extinguished by my own disbelief.

Four

Home

There is a house in my mind that looks like the one I grew up in. It sits back into the desert, detached from real estate, from reality, a terraced house wanting a terrace. It's smaller than I remember. But then it wasn't perched on the edge of a void last time I saw it. Not that it's entirely out of place. The northern industrial town I'm from sometimes felt like this. Like I was always one misstep from being swallowed by the abyss.

We walk towards the house along a ridge. The earth falls away steeply on both sides, so far that clouds have formed in the space they've left, an ocean of inverted sky stretching out into the dark. By moonlight the effect is eerie, as if we're walking on clouds.

In the silence, shadows detach from the night sky and swoop overhead.

I say: *Are those—*
Jon says: *Bats.*

Up close the house is out of place, in disrepair, ripped right from the street it sat on. The sandstone brick is jagged like a mouth with missing teeth. Wallpaper and bathroom fittings from neighbouring houses sit intact on the outer walls. Mains water sprays from a broken pipe.

As we approach the front door, Jon pulls a knife from his boot, starts carving something on the wall. I ask what he's doing. *Checking for damp*, he says, flashing me the kind of grin that says he's up to mischief. He turns back to his work and a minute later walks away. *Come on*, he says, *time's ticking*. He enters without knocking. I stop to read what he's inscribed on the stone. Two simple words: *YOUR MOM*. Up ahead I hear Jon laugh to himself like a giddy schoolgirl.

I'm seven, climbing through a grate in the floor at the front of our house. It's late at night and we've locked ourselves out. The house is old enough to have a coal cellar, and I'm the only one small enough to squeeze through. Later I'll love being here alone. But now it's dark, cold. Foreign. The terror of dancing shadows and strange sounds gives way to curiosity, then calm. I take the key from the kitchen, unlock the back door, feeling the house get smaller with every step.

I'm fourteen, home sick from school. I decide to light a candle, nearly burn the house down. My dad is furious. I don't know how to tell him it was comforting, right up to the point I dropped it on to the carpet, melted several holes into the pile. He managed to fix it so you couldn't tell. Years later I found out he replaced the whole carpet without telling me.

The door of the house in my mind is painted green, chips at the edges showing the colours it used to be: blue, red, green again. The doors of my childhood. I follow Jon inside, but it's no longer the same house. As I walk, the halls and rooms shift and blur. Doors and walls from different houses I've lived in, dreams of houses I never will. I strike the wall with my fist like this is 'Take On Me', and the decor settles on wood chip, because little says childhood like wood chip.

Up ahead Jon is shutting doors, shaking his head. I ask if he's looking for the can. He shuts another door. *An exit*, he says. I'm about to suggest we just use the door we came through but I turn around to see it isn't there any more.

There are things I'd tell her, if she were here now: *I'm sorry. I didn't mean it to end like this.*

I open a door and I'm in the bedroom of my student house, a chaos of crockery and spent clothing, none of it clean. Inside I'm twenty-one, sitting at my desk, working on my first novel. The book is like *Fight Club* but with karaoke – gangs of disaffected men, starved of emotional outlets, engaging in underground singing competitions. I watch myself write a while. I'm younger, leaner. I haven't thought about this book in years. I wrote in a fever, finished the first draft in eight weeks. It won acclaim from my tutors but a girl I was seeing at the time told me she hated it. I put it in a drawer and never took it out again. I shut the door and grip my notebook tight.

We went to university in the same city, different schools. We'd never met at the time. Turns out we'd been at some of the same gigs, stood in the same rooms. We had mutual friends on Facebook. I was at the more prestigious school. I'd remind her of this as often as possible. Sometimes she'd remind me that she got a first-class degree. That she also has a Masters. Sometimes I'd remind her that she thought black comedy meant Kenan and Kel.

The book I'm writing now is about a burned-out eighties rock star who by the mid-nineties is an addict with porcelain teeth and a deviated septum. After breaking out of rehab in LA, he sets out on a road trip back home to New Jersey. His name is Johnny Electric. The book is named after him.

Some prisons have wood chip. The house I grew up in had two floors, maybe fifty feet deep. Here the hallway stretches far enough to become a dot, a thousand doors and none of them an exit. Jon joins me in the hall, slamming a door behind him. *I don't know whose bathroom that is, but they're out of paper,* he says. He leans back against the door. *You ever wipe your ass with a moist towelette.* I don't answer. *Heaven,* he says. I don't have time. I try door after door: hotels, hovels, couches I've crashed on. The further I walk the more closed-in the hall feels. Suddenly I'm slamming doors with barely contained fury. Jon keeps pace behind me. *I'm telling you, champ, you haven't lived until you've cleaned your asshole with a wet wipe.*

Jon is singing. He smells of whiskey. I ask if he's going to help. *Doing everything for you doesn't help,* he says. I ask if he's drunk. He laughs. *I mean, I'm not undrunk.* I open a door, slam it. He tells me I take things too seriously. *Well, at least I exist,* I say. He goes quiet.

Hey man, he says. *I exist.*
I know, buddy, I say.

It turns out if you're careless with your words you can hurt Jon Bon Jovi's feelings after all.

I'm six years old, covering the walls of my room in rub-on transfer letters, the kind you buy in craft shops. It seems like a great idea. My parents don't agree. They ground me for a month. I spend it scraping small black letters from the wood chip. Life is consequences.

Some doors demand to be opened. This door has a hand-drawn sign pinned to it. *Leave me alone.* My childhood bedroom.

Inside the room is small, smaller, a single bed in the corner, two sash windows overlooking the back garden. I don't remember what colour the carpet was. It keeps shifting under my feet, unable to place itself. I sit in the middle of the room, younger me, playing with toys. I must be eight, nine. My hair was still blond, then. I'm wearing four T-shirts, something I did when I was cold. I don't know why I didn't just wear a jumper. Without looking up, my younger self hands me a toy. *Here,* he says. It's an anthropomorphic dog wearing futuristic battle armour. His name is Shakes, he's a Tomorrow Knight. I sit with myself on the carpet. *We're making parachutes for them,* he says. Suddenly I'm trying to tie knots with wet eyes.

Tomorrow Knights were teenage anthropomorphised dogs from the future who travelled back in time to present-day London in order to prevent global warming. They were knights, complete with swords and mechanical horses. Each had a distinct personality and a different fighting style. They listened to Punk and New Wave, which was the only music left in their time. They were named after famous English writers: Sir Shakespeare, Lady Austen, Sir Blake, Lady Woolf. Their mentor was an owl named Dante. It was much better than the other mutant animal shows – *Biker Mice from Mars*, *Street Sharks*, the *Turtles* – to me, at least. Corey Haim did one of the voices. The show ended in 1991. I got my first Bon Jovi record a year later.

I watch as he, younger me, cuts lengths of string from a spool, diligently lays them out next to his toy. He hands the spool to me. *You have to cut them like this,* he says. He ties a length of string to each corner of a handkerchief, and then ties the other end of the string to the wrists and knees of the toy. I follow his lead, fumbling with the knots, less because of the size of my hands, more because I'm out of practice. He shows me how to fold the handkerchief, how to hold it so it doesn't tangle. My hands remember. *Come on*, he says, standing up, walking to the window. We open one each and lean out. I have to kneel. *Throw it up*, he says. *As high as you can. Then the parachute has time to open.* I nod. He counts. *One. Two. Three.* Our brave Knights tumble upward, the handkerchiefs unravelling, catching the air as the toys apex. Both slowly fall towards the back garden. *We have to fetch them*, he says. I look at Jon, standing in the doorway. He taps a watch he isn't wearing. I apologise to myself, promise to come back. He sits on the carpet, nods. *That's okay*, he says. I want to tell him I'll stay longer next time, but I've already closed the door.

Cute kid, Jon says. *Whatever happened to him.*

I'm nine, on a family holiday. I leave my Tomorrow Knights on the beach overnight. *They won't be there tomorrow*, Mum says. I don't believe her. The next morning they're gone. In the night the sea crept up and stole them. Life is consequences.

Five

Home, Part II

Jon makes a dramatic production of choosing a door, pressing his palms together and using his fingertips as a divining rod. He pushes it open and we step in. It's my flat in London. My unconscious body lies in the middle of the studio, a single room that is the bedroom, living room and kitchen. The bathroom is separate. I moved here to get some space. To get some writing done. Turns out I didn't get much of either.

He kicks my comatose form. I wince at the sight. I look terrible, like pizza dough left to prove. There is a wrap of Ketamine open on my desk. A blister pack of pills lies on the floor, the faux-wood laminate scattered with dishes, with my hulking frame. A half-finished bowl of cereal sits soggy on the counter. Sometimes I have as many as six suicidal thoughts before breakfast.

The flat is cramped, and there are books packed in anywhere they'll fit. Two tall shelves filled to bursting. Books in drawers. Books in the kitchen cupboards. Books in the oven. I never used it. I joked about putting books in the bath for the same reason. It smells of freon and misery.

I say: *I thought I'd be happy here.*
Jon says: *Happiness isn't a place.*

It's my thirty-first birthday and we're at karaoke, her treat. She set rules: Emo only, and you can't choose your own song. We're half a dozen drinks deep, voices shot. No sign of slowing down. It's her turn. 'You're So Last Summer' by Taking Back Sunday. Midway through a waiter arrives with our drinks. She takes a large white wine from the tray, downs it in the vocal break, sets the glass back down, calmly asks the waiter for another, picks up the song without missing a beat. I walk over, kiss her. *I love you*, I say. It's the first time I've said that. She smiles, asks me to tell her again. I take the microphone. *I love you*, I say. *I love you. I love you. I love you.*

I tell people that's when I realised I loved her but that isn't true. The day I knew, she'd woken up sick, full of flu. I dressed her in my finest warmery, went out to get Lemsip, Sudafed, soup. She was so cute when she was sick. Things had been pretty casual between us, but suddenly all I wanted was to look after her. We binged on *Parks and Rec*. Read books. Napped. As she snuggled up, slept off the fever, I melted entirely, finally admitted to myself I was hopelessly in love.

On the wall of my one room home is a cork board with a US map pinned to it. The basic outline of my novel scrawled across in black marker pen, little more than a series of dots with a line between. *Not much of a plan*, Jon says, flipping through my notebook. I take it off him. *It'll get me where I need to go*, I say. He walks to the bathroom, pisses with the door open. *Speaking of needing to go*, he says. *Damn whiskey dropped right through me.*

Johnny Electric is what Jon almost called his band, before he changed his name and used that. I'm glad he did. It's an awful name for a band, but it's a half-decent name for a book.

There are notes pinned to the board, too. Scene. Chunks of dialogue. Title ideas. Things she said. The latter notes aren't for the novel. They're there just to remind me not to text her. *I love you. Don't make this difficult. I'm not attracted to you any more.* It doesn't always work.

In the microwave are a stack of self-help books I hid when I had people over. I pick one up, thumb through it. Well-meaning words arranged in pleasing ways across the page. It's not long before all you see are empty epithets, aphorisms that carry only the illusion of wisdom. Idioms with the nutritional value of a microwave meal. An apt hiding place, then.

Even before she left, I devoted a lot of time to wondering how to be. How to talk, how to dress. *Do people laugh like this, and the way I'm sitting, is this one of the accepted ways.* I bought books that promised to explain, to unlock secrets, truths. Books that would make me better. Everything studied. Every thought, every action interrogated. It never occurred to me to just be.

Novel idea: A gritty reboot of children's classic, *Not Now, Bernard.*

Any book is a self-help book, if you read it right.

Jon takes a red pen from the jar on my desk. Having lots of pens makes me feel like a writer. He bites the cap off the marker, places a dot in California, another in Nevada, draws a line between the two. He looks at me, the coolest substitute teacher you never had. *I said think of this place like a map, right.* I nod. *We started in California, drove clean across a desert, and now we're here.* He points to the Nevada dot. *We had five days,* he says. *We've got four left.* He slides his hand across the map, puts the pen down on the East Coast. New York. *And this is where we have to get to.* He points to my supine mass. *Or the bunny gets it.* He tosses the pen on the desk, bows. *So what next,* I say. He opens a single malt, fills his flask. *Fucked if I know.*

I'm fifteen, trying to write a novel. It's a retelling of Robin Hood, but set in a *Blade Runner*-like future. I give up after the first paragraph. Years later I'll read that a new Robin Hood film is in production, one set in the future. Like *Blade Runner*. I'll tell everyone Hollywood is stealing my ideas. Eventually I realise an idea you don't use doesn't belong to you at all.

Novel idea: A man takes a road trip through his own mind with Jon Bon Jovi.

Where I'm from, if you want to insult a stranger, you call them *Johnny Something*. A guy with a Mohawk you'd say, *Who does Johnny Haircut think he is.* A guy who walks like he owns the street is *Johnny Big Bollocks*. A guy who fucks everything up, well. You get the idea.

If she were here now I'd apologise and I'd have no idea what for. I never listened. *I'm sorry. Don't make this difficult. I'm not attracted to you any more.*

You never use her name, he says.
I know, I say. *Hurts to say it.*

I study the map, ask why we have four days. *You know why,* he says. *You won't last longer than that.* I look at my body. Puffy, pale. I could be dead already. *And New York,* I say. He shrugs, pulls the door open. *All I know is that's where this ends,* he says. *Guess it's just that kind of story.*

My book is about a singer road-tripping across America in search of himself. Jon took a trip like that once, but the book isn't about Jon. It's about me, about a trip I took. Me and Paul and a minivan named Gary Busey. We never finished it.

Johnny See. Johnny Do. Johnny Ruin.

I follow Jon into the hall. The heels of his boots click like a metronome on the hardwood. I asked for this. To be here. But this isn't home. It's a storage unit, that's all. A place I keep places. I do this when things get hard. Run, hide. But Jon's right. I need to finish this. Even if I die trying.

I want to fix it, I say. *Fix me.*
To get her back, he says.
To get me back, I say.
Good. That's good.
Shall we begin.
Already did.

The end of the hallway rushes to meet us, only it's not an end. It's a fire door, a red exit sign glows above it. Jon takes my arm. *There are parts of your brain that'll try to stop you*, he says. *Further we go, deeper we travel, harder this gets.* He lets go. *I know*, I say.

I push the door open and step into the darkness beyond.

Six

Nevada / Lust

The dark carries an electric hum and the smell of rain. We step into an alley, a cavern of concrete and neon-bathed brick. Graffiti crawls across the stone: *abandon all clothes, ye who enter*. Vast buildings rise into the clouds, piercing the night. Phallic towers of glass clad in the kind of electronic billboards you'd find in Vegas. Here, they're filled with filth. Everywhere I look is wall-to-wall smut, an array of single-minded depravity. All of it mine.

Jon points at a video screen hanging high above us. *That your Johnson*, he says. The screen broadcasts a dick pic, forty feet tall, in high definition. I nod. He stares a little longer. *That angle does you a lot of favours.*

I don't remember my first hard-on. There must have been a first. No doubt triggered by something inappropriate. Hard-ons are mostly inappropriate, almost always inconvenient.

The first time I masturbated I thought I'd broken something. It was a willy, back then, when these things were discussed in whispers and euphemisms. I ran to the bathroom to check it wasn't damaged, scared I'd have to tell my parents. I was ten. I'd just found my new favourite toy. I didn't play with action figures much after that.

My twenty-two-year-old self walks past with a girl we'd just met. I turn to watch him, me, kissing her against a wall in the alley. I hitch her skirt up, pull down her tights, and push a hand into her knickers. She braces herself against the wall and groans loudly enough that I place my other hand over her mouth. She buries her face in my palm, comes, knees buckling slightly, before reaching for my belt. I don't remember her name. I'm not sure I ever got it, but I remember her orgasm, her body shuddering against me. Katrina, maybe. I think I made a joke about waves.

We walk without purpose, eyes pulled in every direction. It's an entire city of red lights. Flesh and vice and all things nice. A sprawl of smut set deep in the darkest seams of my subconscious. The streets are lined with floor-to-ceiling windows, lit by neon, each holding a memory, a fantasy, a kink. Glass-clad buildings scrape the sky, each room filled with lurid things I've seen and done. Others are empty, yet waiting for inspiration. This place is the product of every orgasm I've given, received, witnessed. These are temples. Shrines. Spank banks. I've made a lot of deposits. *I don't think this one needs an introduction,* Jon says. *No,* I say. *I know what this is.*

Lust, the other four-letter word.

Is she in here, I say, unable to see the city for the skyscrapers. *In here,* he says. He points up. *She has her own building.* A block away, a single tower rises above the cloud line. A temple. A prison. The same thing, I suppose. Depends which side of the wall you're on.

That night we met I really turned on the charm. I was warm, witty, thought I said a lot of clever things. She laughed along.

Later she told me I was a bit much, but she really wanted to fuck me, so she put up with it. *Don't worry*, she said, *your bullshit is mostly bearable.*

Sample tweet: *Why impress others when you can impress your fence. Buy JoeSeal.*

When we met I couldn't believe she was interested. I waited for her to change her mind, was still surprised when she did. It's not just lights that are extinguished by disbelief.

The worst thing you can say in an argument is *whatever*.

Rain now, dense and unrelenting. Movie rain. Jon and I shelter under the awning of one of the buildings. An electronic ticker runs along the side of the building opposite – the kind that would usually display stock prices or breaking news – thousands of red dots arranged to create a continuous stream of filth I've texted to various people over the years: *What are you wearing. Where are your hands. Show me.*

I'm twenty-two, on my road trip. I've been driving for sixteen hours, fuelled by Red Bull, gas-station bologna, wonder bread. Paul is asleep in back, seats folded into the floor so he can stretch out. It's dark and my mind is racing. I don't know what sets me off. It doesn't take much. Up to now I've been sneaking cheeky wanks in motel showers, but we haven't seen a motel in a week. No bed. No rooms. No privacy. Needs must. I'm doing eighty when I shift the car into cruise. After checking the rear view for signs of consciousness, I reach into my shorts, grab my cock, very slowly pulling and twisting around the head. Normally I'd use my whole hand, but my fingertips will do, focused in the right place, the right rhythm. In a minute I'm rock hard and throbbing, cock hot with blood, friction. I keep one hand on the wheel and two eyes on the road. It's automatic. Auto-erotic. Within two minutes my whole body locks up and I struggle to keep the wheel straight as I come, the car drifting sideways across the blacktop. I pull over a few minutes later to change my boxers. It never occurred to me to pull over for a wank in the first place.

That thing where a loose paving slab splashes water all over your trailing foot.

Jesus-Fuck-Christmas is what Jon says, getting used to life with a wet boot.

The second worst thing you can do in an argument is laugh.

We step out into the street, narrowly avoiding a swerving minivan with my distracted twenty-one-year-old self at the wheel. *Not the stupidest thing you've done with your dick,* he says. *Not even top three.*

I remember my notebook, snatch it from my back pocket. The cover is damp but the pages, the words, aren't damaged. I'm only wearing a T-shirt. *Fuck.* I tuck it under my arm. *Wallet,* Jon says. I blink at him. *Got a rubber, don't you.* I catch on, pull out my wallet, find the condom I keep there. I wind my notebook into a tight column, tear open the condom packet with my teeth, rolling the thin film over the paper, tip to hilt, before pinching the end and tying it in a knot. *Never used that much condom before,* I say. *Didn't realise they cover so much notebook.* Jon grins as I push the latex-wrapped notebook into my back pocket. *Not the worst thing you've done with a condom, either.*

We don't rush to find another awning. There's no need. The temperature is steady. Twenty-two degrees. Besides, I love the rain. There's a word for that. I think it's made up. But then, they all are.

We used to go clothes shopping together. We'd buy things for her. Dresses, shoes. Lingerie. I'd sit, wait patiently, overheat. She'd model things for me. I'm not even a foot guy, but her feet in anything pointy, heely, made me salivate. It was foreplay, imagining hitching up that dress, that skirt. We'd both get so turned on. Most times we'd go straight home, where I'd strip her slowly from the new wares. Sometimes she'd keep them on. The latter tended to make returns difficult.

Here, through a window, I watch her trying on a dress she isn't sure about, one I chose. I knew she'd look stunning in it. She does. She poses for me, turning, pouting, laughing. Her hair pulled back in a ponytail. Her pale limbs, long and lithe, pull curious poses. My very own model. Her very own adoring fan. My smile fades as the curtain closes and I'm left looking at my reflection. I'm already walking away. There's more to see.

In a window a little further down the block she's making me breakfast in one of my Bon Jovi T-shirts and not much else. It was my birthday. Underneath the T-shirt is a pair of lace knickers, my favourites. She can see me in her periphery, hovering, lingering, unable to look away. This is all for me. She'd asked me what I wanted for my thirty-first. This is the result. When she's satisfied she's got my attention, she drops a spoon, makes a show of picking it up. She wipes her mouth with the bottom of the T-shirt, showing me her knickers. Through the fabric I get a glimpse of her cunt, where her labia meet at the top, a dark patch of hair perched above. She knows this drives me crazy. She pulls the shirt up far enough to flash me her tits, then drops it, teasing. The grin on her face reserved just for me. She notices Jon, standing behind me. He's also staring.

He says: *Aren't you supposed to be fixing yourself.*
I say: *Aren't you supposed to be fetching a car.*
He says: *Aren't you supposed to be listening.*

We turn to each other. *I'm listening.* In my periphery I can see she's pouting. *We need to leave*, he says, *we're only here to get to the next place.* He leans back against the glass, puts one foot against it, tips the rain from the brim of his hat. *Shit. You spend way too much time here as it is.* I tell him maybe I'm here to work on that. To figure it out. He shakes his head. *You're not going to fix yourself standing here, staring at her funfair. You know where we need to be, and it ain't Disneyland.* I nod like I'm listening but what I'm actually doing is walking to the next window.

She's in the bathtub, pale, water-draped, pristine skin dancing in candlelight. Wet hair falls over her shoulders and chest, finding her nipples red, raised. Her pubic bone crests slightly. Her hip bones stand sharp, inviting my hands, my teeth. Her torso sits up on her elbows, head falling back towards me. Her eyes are closed. Her lips are parted slightly, just enough to kill me. My hands start at her neck, pulling her hair back into a ponytail. I move down the whole length, working the soap to a lather. I'm clumsy, unused to washing more than my own close crop. I haven't used enough shampoo, but she is patient as I reach for more. I take a cup and carefully pour water from her hairline down the length, then wring the hair to rinse fully before starting over with conditioner. The scene smells like my pillows after she spends the night.

Even now I can smell her there, on my pillows.

Even though the scent is long gone.

I lay her head back on the tub, and she lowers herself into the water, resting her hands on her thighs. Starting just above her ears, I bridge my fingertips and draw them up to her crown, scraping lightly over her scalp. She moans, rolls her shoulders, tilting her head as I move. I let my fingers interlock then pull them apart, moving them in slow circles. I start small, digging deep then softly scraping, massaging then scratching. Her breathing is deep, each circle eliciting a groan. The firmer my fingers, the harder I scratch, the deeper her sigh. The water sloshes as she writhes, her thighs tensing together and hips rocking upward as I work her slowly, every scrape of my nails over her scalp prompting a *fuckkkk*, a moan, a shudder. As I finish, her eyes still closed, she whispers six words that echo through me: *You make me feel so good.*

In reality, out there, back then, it didn't quite play out like this. I did a poor job, blamed the angle, the bathtub. She ended up doing it herself. I prefer to remember it this way.

I rinse her hair three times, then a fourth when she says it's not done yet. She stands and steps out of the bath, where I wrap her in a warm towel. She kisses me, rests her head on my chest. We stay like that a moment until I feel her shiver. *Shall we find you some warm clothes,* I say. She sniffs and nods, the way a child might. We exit, pursued by a stare. A minute later, the scene resets. Jon and I watch as she strips and gets into the bath, wetting her hair before calling me in.

The ticker trails above us: *Show me. Show me. Show me. Show me. Show me. Show me. Sho—*

Rain patters the window. Beads of water drip from my hair, run down my forehead. Rinse and repeat. *Something hurts that much,* Jon says, *best thing is to stop doing it.* I wipe my brow. *Maybe I like the pain.* He turns away and faces the street. *Maybe you like it too much,* he says. Through the glass I watch her lips, waiting. *Just a minute,* I say. I want to hear it one more time.

Her: *You make me feel so good.*

Come on, he says. *We've already been here too long. Places to be, champ.* But I'm not listening. I'm stumbling, lust drunk, lost in her. I step off the pavement into the road. The electric hum grows louder. Street lights surge and shatter, throwing yellow sparks over the water-logged asphalt, like it's raining fire. And then there is only her. She steps towards me from every direction. She's on every billboard, in every window. Her curves, her groans, her whispers. *Stop this,* Jon says. But I can't. I don't want to. She's in summer dresses. In lingerie. In my Bon Jovi T-shirt and nothing else. She's in a bath towel. She's naked. Rain soaked. I follow the curve of her hips, the tussock of hair above her cunt. Then higher: her tits, her neck, her lips, her eyes, her hair. Sophia. I'm hers and she knows. I turn again to find her in jeans, a T-shirt. I feel the sharp sting of her hand across my cheek. *I told you,* she says, *I don't want you thinking of me like this.*

Jon's laughter rises above the ringing in my ears, my face burning where her hand kissed it.

Seven

Nevada / Lust, Part II

The first time we kissed she pressed her body into mine, my hand sliding from her hips to her lower back, around her arse, between her legs, until my fingers could feel the heat through her knickers. She pressed her hips forward, her pubic bone pushing against my cock. Then I remembered we were standing in a busy club. Every second with her I was carried away.

From that first kiss we existed only in a bubble, our entire world extending outward three feet in every direction, wrapped around us like a duvet.

Later, when it's over, she'll say something that haunts me still: *It never would have lasted.*

Wait, I say. *Wait.* It sounds more pathetic the second time. She's already leaving, all of her. The Sophia who slapped me, the one in the jeans and T-shirt, leading a revolution away from me. A revolt. Revolting. They're all dressed now, dressed like her. *I can't turn it off,* I say. She stops. *Then we can't be friends.* I ask her where she's going, then: *Don't leave.*

On a video billboard she's in a changing room, showing me a dress she's trying on. She's hitched it up so the hem is above her hips. She isn't wearing knickers. A picture she sent me once. She looks up, shakes her head. *I'm not going to stick around and play love interest,* she says. *Fuck that.* She turns a corner. It's been a year since we last kissed. Last fucked. We're not friends. We can't be friends for a lot of reasons. One is that I can't turn this off. Another is that she's with someone else. *That went well,* Jon says, chewing a toothpick he pulled out of thin air.

On another screen, Sophia is masturbating in a bathroom stall. We were at a restaurant, drunk, horny. She got up to go to the bathroom and I asked her to send me something. I got this video. She's leaning against the wall, her skirt hitched up, hand in her knickers. She asked me to delete it when she broke things off. She asked me to delete everything I had. Pictures, videos. And I did. I didn't need them. On the screen above, her legs tense and she rubs her clit harder, whispering. *Fuck, I'm gonna come.* I can't delete memories. They play on a continuous loop in my head. On screen she adjusts her skirt, blows a kiss into camera, and the video begins again.

Jon says: *Where are you going.*
I say: *After her, obviously.*
Jon says: *She said not to.*
I say: *Didn't stop me before.*
Jon says: *That's not strictly true.*

I always liked the pain of mouth ulcers, probing them with my tongue till they bled.

I lean back against the glass, see things from his point of view. The road is a river, heavy rain flows into the gutter, over the kerb. American streets with their small drains, adverse camber. Good for flooding pavements, little else. Jon sighs. *We could always swim out of here.*

Ahead, a raised track winds between buildings. *You know how to get to Magic Mountain*, I say. *You take the train.* I can't see any trains from here, but an absence of trains doesn't mean one isn't coming. Keep the faith, as they say.

You wait long enough by a train track, you tend to find a train.

We follow the track. Still the rain falls. Still the water rises, surface black as the sky above it. Reflected neon flickers as raindrops break the surface, warping the inverted words. A city drowning in sin. A sewer swimming in itself. Literally. Jon is bracing himself against a wall, writing his name in piss on the stone. He holds his dick in one hand and lifts his flask to his lips with the other. Not the water cycle you learned about in school. He goes to the bathroom more than any human or non-corporeal travelling companion I've ever met.

He walks backward as he pisses, attempting to outrun the expanding pool of urine floating on the rainwater. He steps back off the kerb and flails to catch himself, overcompensating and almost ending up with a face full of piss. *Think you've had enough to drink there*, I say, moving away from him. *Certainly not*, he says, buttoning his fly. He pushes his flask into his back pocket, accepting that pissing in water he's standing in was probably a bad idea.

The track is directly above us, but stairs prove elusive. I turn a corner into a side street. It's darker here. Most of the street lights are out and the ones that aren't flicker on and off. Mostly off. *Track's that-a-way*, Jon says. I don't look where he points. *Yes*, I say. *It is.*

We should've been long gone by now.
I told you. I say. *I need to find her.*
This storm ain't a coincidence.
We don't leave without her.
And if she don't want to.

Up ahead I'm twenty-three, fucking a girl I don't know over the bonnet of my car. Her knickers are round her knees. I'm pulling her ponytail and she keeps saying, *Harder, harder.* I can't go any harder. I'm tempted to ask her to pipe down so I can concentrate. The strobing effect of the street light turns the scene into a zoetrope, our staccato thrusts rendered like nineteenth-century porn.

In a window across the street I'm seventeen going down on a girl for the first time and getting it all incredibly wrong. She's good enough to humour me, lets me stumble around her labia for a long while until I ask her if she came and she can't help but laugh.

We walk past my thirty-two-year-old self apologising to a date for not being able to get a hard-on. I offer to go down on her again but she tells me that it's okay. She puts a hand on my shoulder. From across the street I watch myself shrink. What I should have done is laughed about it. *What you should have done,* Jon says, *is used a finger as a splint. Just until the blood starts pumping.* I walk away. *What,* he says. *Don't say you've never thumbed-in a semi.*

The thing with pain is it lets you know you exist. Sometimes pushing your tongue into an open wound in your mouth is the only way to be sure.

You think maybe it's time to retire this place, Jon says. *It's not good for you.* The water is knee deep. I wade on. *It's not healthy, you know. Dwelling on this stuff.* We walk by a dark window where I can just about make out my form, pressed to the wall, wanking to the sound of someone else fucking. *I know, I know,* I say. *I just need to find her.* He stops. *I don't think that's going to be a problem,* he says, nodding at the space behind me.

They shuffle from the shadows, sloshing in knee deep water. Dozens of her. A hundred, maybe, in various states of dress. They inch closer, calling out to me. They tear at their own clothing, claw at mine. Jon pulls me towards him, we back up against the building behind us. *What's the matter,* they say. *Don't you want me.* Their mouths all curl in a grin, the one she reserves for me.

We need an exit, Jon says, making a half jump for a second-storey window ledge. No dice. A Sophia dressed as a nurse grabs my T-shirt and pulls me in for a kiss, and for a moment I let her as another grabs my hair and pulls hard enough to rip some out.

I push away nurse Sophia as another hand reaches for my belt. There's a hand on my arse, I feel my notebook start to leave my back pocket, snatch it back. I have hands up my shirt, fingers in my mouth. *Make me feel good,* she says, pulling my hand between her legs. *Come on, buddy, exit,* Jon says, wrestling his hat away from one of her. My T-shirt rips. Lust will tear us apart.

There is no exit, I say, doing my best to rebuckle my belt, stop my jeans sliding off. *There's always an exit,* Jon says. As he does, the double doors behind us swing open. Sophia, the Sophia who slapped me, grabs both of us, pulls us inside.

I got married at twenty-five. Partly a visa thing. Seemed like a good idea at the time. We loved each other. We just didn't like each other very much. As stories go, it was a hatchet job of a love plot, rushed, clichéd. I thought I could fix it later. I couldn't. By twenty-eight, it had collapsed at the end of the first act.

By thirty I was adrift, stumbling between beds, bottles. Enter Sophia. She was a revelation. Newly single, not looking for anything. We found each other at a time when we didn't know what we needed, and made that thing each other. The thing with bubbles is that they tend to burst.

It's good to give your character some kind of disability to overcome. In my book, years of substance abuse has left Johnny Electric all but impotent.

I can't remember a girl who's got me hard since her.

Those doors won't hold for long, she says. I ask how she knows, but she's already taken off running. *Because you don't want them to,* she says. We're in the kind of service corridor you get behind the scenes in a mall, all concrete floors, white walls.

The fists of a hundred memories bear down on the doors behind us. *Why are you helping,* I say, wheezing. Jon and I are struggling with the pace. *I'm not,* she says, *you're helping me.* She pushes out of another set of double doors on to a train platform.

We're a storey above the city streets. She closes the door, drags a metal bench in front of it. I help. I like to feel useful. *You really want to be useful,* she says. *You can conjure a train. I've been waiting a year for one to show up.*

Across from the street we can see into a row of windows. Some I used to see from the overground train. One I used to live opposite. In each, people are undressing. Women, men. Strangers, giving glimpses of underwear, of bare skin. She speaks without looking at me. *You fetishise your memories.* I watch as they all close curtains, blinds. *Don't all writers,* I say.

A man at the other end of the platform now. I can't see who it is. His face shifts like the carpet of my childhood bedroom, unable to place itself. He stares me down. Her boyfriend, maybe. The one she's seeing now. The one she was seeing before we met. It's hard to tell. He could be anyone. An identikit, photofit, simulacrum of a man I've wronged. There are others with him. Other wrongs. Other regrets. They charge at us, shouting. The Sophias batter the double doors behind us. We stand, start down the platform. *Call a train,* she says, but I don't know how. We're being hunted by my mistakes. My legs are leaden. I'm usually faster than this.

Jon is panting. *Anytime you want to deal with this, you have my full support,* he says. Sophia is at the end of the platform. I catch up with her. We look over the rail. A forty-foot drop into the rising water below. No distance left to run. *There,* she says, pointing to a fire escape.

She hits the rungs, not waiting for us. I make room for Jon to go next, but he pushes me towards the ladder. *Anytime now,* he says. As the mob reach the middle of the platform the double doors slam open and a hundred Sophias spill out, swarming my wrongs. Jon hauls himself on to the ladder. *What's the collective noun for that.*

If you really want to fuck someone up, love them as hard as you can.

The rain is relentless, and the rungs of the ladder are slippery when wet. A mist has descended over the city, and visibility is down to a few feet. I can't see Sophia, but I can hear Jon: *Is it still a fire escape if there's no fire, or is it just an escape.*

I top out, climb on to the tarred felt. A thick fog caps the building. I shout into the storm but the wind picks up, batters me with rain. I'm leaning forward just to stay upright. The fog only seems to get thicker. Jon finds me, grabs my shoulder. *And for your next trick,* he says. I'm not sure it's a trick, but the mist parts in front of us to reveal a train carriage sitting on a second set of tracks.

Wait long enough for a train and it doesn't come, maybe you're by the wrong damn tracks.

The last time I saw her she was across the room at a party, wearing a dress she'd bought out shopping with me. I drank three glasses of champagne, went over to speak to her. By the time I got there my words had slid back down my throat. I managed only a nod before her attentions were stolen away by someone who'd never loved her. That was two weeks ago.

The last time I thought of her, I'd woken to a hard-on and a memory of her straddling my face, her hips rocking as my tongue made her come. In the waste land of my bed I could practically taste her. The moment I came I knew I'd fucked up. I'd been sober for thirty days.

As Jon and I approach, the train doors slide open. Sophia stands in the doorway. *Tear it down,* she says. She nods at the cityscape behind us, towers of glass rising high into the night, a red neon constellation sprawling miles in every direction.

On the adjacent building, a video billboard eighty feet high shows Sophia leaning into the camera, naked, writhing, her lips mouthing three words over and over. I don't need to hear it to know what she's saying. It's written on a vintage sign on the opposite roof, letters two storeys tall and lit with neon bulbs: *I'm gonna come.*

Tear it down, she says. *Or you're not getting on this train.* I walk to the next door. Sophia beats me there. *Tear it down.* I try again, she runs to stop me. I try to barge past. She places her palms on my chest, pushes with enough force to stop me. *No.* Jon's hand on my shoulder now. *You're better than this,* he says. I can't look him in the eye. *This is all I have left,* I say. Sophia steps forward, takes my hand. She leans right in, whispers in my ear. *Tear it down.*

When I was seven a girl in the schoolyard dropped her knickers, let the boys see her downstairs bits. We recoiled in horror, ran away laughing. Six years later in high school, we were all begging to get in her knickers. She had absolutely no interest.

I'm twenty-two, fucking a one-night stand. I tell her I love how wet she is. *Well,* she says, *you would be too if you were walking round with an open cavity into your body.*

I close my eyes, clench my fists. The wind rips at my rain-soaked shirt. Jon and Sophia stand back. Around me lights flicker then explode, cascading sparks falling like fireworks. The scaffolding behind the giant letters buckles as bulbs pop like electric balloons. The sign groans, tips forward, stripping its bolts, falling over the edge to the city below. In an adjacent building, glass windows start to shatter, steel beams melt like butter, entire floors blow out, collapse. I open my eyes and watch the city crumble. Like the forest before it. Like the cars on the highway. I crash the memory. Destroy it. Tear it down. Jon moves towards the train, *Come on.*

From the dark a hand reaches out, grabs my ankle. I look down to see a man without a face, a flat red pulp where the face is meant to be. Paul. He reaches out to grab my other leg and I stumble, fall back. He crawls up my body, peers down at me. I try to push him off, but there's no strength in my arms. My fingers press into the raw flesh of his unface. The stump of his tongue darts around as he speaks. *Remember those birds we picked up at the karaoke.*

His blood drips into my mouth. I spit it out, thick, ferric. Jon is trying to pull him off me. *Yours was all right*, he says. *Mine though, fanny like a wizard's sleeve.* He coughs a blood-choked laugh as Jon pulls me clear. The roof is shaking violently. We run for the train, squeeze through the closing doors. I turn to see Paul's faceless body reaching out into the dark as the roof collapses beneath him. From the window I watch as the city falls.

Out there, in the world. I've lost her.

Here, she's standing next to me.

The rest is lust and detritus.

Eight

Colorado / Obsession

Set the scene. Mountains, lakes, trees. A thousand postcards stitched together paint a vivid cinescape, their seams visible, overlapping. Above, the sky is a hundred swatches of the same blue. A panorama of Pantone cards. The carriage I'm in moves through this collage at 150 miles an hour. I know this because Jon tells me, his face pressed against the window as we traverse a viaduct that shouldn't be here. He has a hard-on for trains.

Outside, a small action figure falls through the air under a handkerchief parachute.

Sophia sits opposite, silent, sullen. I can't look at her. My shoulders hunched, breath shallow. I'm all knots. Sheepshank stomach. Half-hitch heart. I'm trying not to tremble. Jon speaks, his breath fogging the glass. *Could be worse,* he says. *This could be really fucking awkward.*

A thing I was into for a while was the BASE Fatality List. It's a website, a chronological record of every BASE jumper killed since 1981. It's a list of names with a date and a paragraph about the jump, what went wrong. I read each new entry with a twisted fascination. Vicarious suicide.

My notebook is unrolled in front of me, pen in hand, condom discarded. I scribble in the margins of a page I haven't written yet. She looks at me across the table and asks what I'm doing. I tell her I'm writing a book. *Looks like you're avoiding writing a book.* I take a breath. Tell her most writing is avoiding writing. It doesn't sound as clever out loud. *What's it about*, she says. *Him.* She looks at Jon. I shake my head. *Ghosts*, I say. She puts in her headphones. *Same thing.*

What you already know about Sophia is that she sees right through you.

I'm thirty. We're on a train together. She pulls my hand between her legs and rocks herself to orgasm against my fingers, letting her hips roll with the carriage. She comes with a slow shudder, her body rigid, expertly turning her satisfied groan into a whole body yawn. Afterwards, she gazes quietly out of the window, kissing my hand in thanks. Nobody notices.

Stop it, Sophia says.
Stop what, I say.
You know.

My eyes drift from her hips to my notes. An unseen conductor makes an announcement over the speaker: *Remember when she said they were just friends.*

That feeling someone is staring at you. I look up to see Sophia's face locked in a mock grimace: eyes wide, nose scrunched, nostrils flared. I don't know how long she's been holding the pose, but I raise my hands to my face and close one eye, clicking the shutter on a camera I'm not holding. She doesn't flinch. I pull a face with less success. She's better at it than me. Less prone to taking herself seriously. Less worried it'll stay that way. She humours me still. I let our eyes meet. Hers, blue glass nebulas. Mine, the Hubble before they fixed it. Compromised. Unable to focus. Danger, Will Robinson. Eject. Eject. I look away quickly, but it's too late. I'm already lost.

The thing about BASE jumping is it's instinct. You stand on top of something, you want to jump off. The call of the void. The French have a phrase for that. The thing about BASE jumping is you have a parachute. It's not suicide if you catch yourself. It's not suicide if you're trying to fly.

The guy who invented BASE jumping also decided to award a sequential number to each person who completed all four BASE jumps: Building, Antennae, Span, Earth. His name was Carl Boenish. He was BASE #4. The fourth man to do all four jumps. He's BASE Fatality #7.

Jon is sleeping. She asks if Bogart was busy. *Elvis too*, I say. *And Eddie Vedder would have brought his ukulele.* That's less a swipe at Eddie Vedder, more a dig at her. Sophia once spent an insufferable month learning the uke.

She furrows her brow. *So now you're stuck with Rex Manning*, she says. *Do you even like his band.*

Jon stirs, shifts in his seat. *I do*, I say. *I used to.*

Announcement: *Remember finding her hair in your bed for months after she left.*

She looks at the loudspeaker, then at me, unimpressed. I try a dozen words, choke on each. *I need some air*, she says, standing. I ask if she's coming back. She frowns. *Do I have a choice.*

I say: *Don't leave.*
She says: *Say it like you mean it.*

The first name on the BASE Fatality List is William Harmon. He died 11 April 1981, jumping from an antenna in Virginia. There's no picture. I like to think he had a moustache, went by Bill.

Sophia is leading. We walk through carriages from different trains: Amtrak, the Tube, Virgin East Coast. I realise my T-shirt is stained with Paul's viscera. I'm a walking Turin shroud of my dead friend. I pull a random bag from the luggage rack and take out a T-shirt, sliding it on over the one I'm already wearing. I don't want to take my shirt off in front of her. Not now.

We pass through a buffet car, tables stacked tall with bagels and pizza and hummus and cheese and chocolate. A feast of foods I binge on. I grab a coffee. The first sip burns my tongue. *Fuck's sake.* She looks at me like I'm a little slow, tells me I can make it any temperature I want. I blow over it. *But if it were the right temperature,* I say, *what would I have to complain about.*

A few carriages later I hear her say, *You fetishise sadness.*

The carriage we're in is a library, the walls lined with books I own. *Have you even read these,* she says. I look at the titles. *Some of them,* I say. She throws me a copy of *The Heart Is Deceitful Above All Things.* Her favourite book. I never finished it. *Not enough,* she says.

We arrive at a bar car, all glower and walnut veneer. It's full of women I've dated, talking among themselves, drinking G&Ts. Sophia takes one from a waiter. *Happy hour,* she says. None of them pay me any attention. It smells like perfume. Like gin and regret.

You dated all these women, she says.
Some of them. Some I've never met.
Then why are they here, she says.
I fall in love a dozen times a day.
That isn't real love, she says.
It's the possibility of love, I say.
Possibilities don't love you back.
I pause a moment. *You did*, I say.

In our bubble, I wake to the slow curve of her shoulder, pale, unsheathed. I trace lines between her moles with the tips of my fingers. Barely touching. She whimpers, rolls her body as I stroke softly, as I hold her halfway between sleep and dream.

In our bubble, she's snoring like a trooper.

Next to me at the bar is a woman I dated long distance. I'd spend all my time saving money to see her. It was fine except when I was with her, when she seemed to resent my presence. Sometimes the best relationships are the ones you imagine.

Sophia points at a woman I had an intense affair with in my early twenties. *What about her*, she says. I tell her to guess. *Your persistence put her off.* She takes another by the shoulders. *You fell for her quickly, then you realised she's a loud eater.* She runs to another. *You hated each other, but the sex was incredible.* I smile. *Two out of three ain't bad.* I don't tell her which two.

She isn't done yet. She runs over to another.
And this one, she says. *She's gorgeous.*

Simple, I say. *She didn't like books.*
And this one. Why did you stop.
Do you want me to be honest.
Brutally, she says. *Always.*
She wasn't you, I say.

In our bubble, we made up terrible insults for each other. Nonsensical stuff. Uninsults. *You're such an ice-cream sandwich,* she says. I gasp in mock outrage. *Bloody cagoule,* I say.

In our bubble, where time found a tempo just for us, there was nothing I loved more than looking over the top of my book to watch her reading hers, waiting for her to feel my gaze. A silent game played until she found a sentence she didn't mind pausing on. The smile I'd get in return, warm enough to linger even now. It's the smile I still see when I close my eyes.

Announcement: *Remember when she broke up with you by text.*

A woman I was sleeping with recently steps in front of me. *You ghosted me,* she says. I tell her that isn't true. It probably is. *You just stopped texting,* she says. She's attractive. I like that Sophia is here to see her. She's also drunk, spilling her gin as she speaks. *Who's this.* She struggles to focus. I introduce Sophia, then I pause. They both look at me. *Are you fucking kidding me,* she says. She introduced herself to Sophia. It's Laura. *Laura,* I say. *The reason I stopped texting is we broke up. I was pretty explicit.* I'm uncomfortable but I don't know how to end this. I already ended it. *You wanna know where guys like you end up,* Laura says. She knocks back the last of her gin, holding up a finger to indicate a pause. *Alone,* I say. She takes another sip of her drink, forgetting she finished it. *You're such a dick.* We watch her leave. Sophia turns to me. *What,* I say.

She raises her glass in a cheers. *You can really dish it out,* she says. *Shame you can't take it.*

Give your character a flaw. A compulsion. Something they can't help. Something that gets them in trouble. Jon wants to be needed. Sophia wants to be liked. Me, I want to be adored.

Come on, she says. She takes my hand, leads me into the next carriage, her hips swaying with the train. I start to ask something, stumble over the words. *What scares you more,* she says, *that my sexual appetite extends beyond you, or that you're having this conversation with yourself.*

We sit on a bench seat in the next carriage, looking through a panoramic window at the mountains of my memory. There is music playing, a Springsteen cover. We sit side by side, staring straight ahead. The peaks rise and fall as we pass, like they're tuned to the wavelength of the song. But the beat is off. I watch them, trying to figure out what doesn't fit. Then it clicks. I feel it in my ribs. Then higher, in my throat. It's my heartbeat. I'm on fire.

Why did you do it, she says. My heart can't help falling over itself, the beats it skips leave gaps between mountains. I ask her why she never texted to ask how I was. *Is it because I moved on,* she says. My heart makes the mountains climb, tumble ever quicker. I ask how hard it is to text. *Were you punishing yourself, or me.* More silence. *Do you ever miss me,* I say. A bull horn blows in the distance. *It's been a year,* she says. I talk to my feet. *And what's one year out of fifty, sixty.* She lifts my chin up. *I can't be here any more.* We rally silence back and forth until I fumble my return. I tell her I'm not ready for her to go. *Shouldn't I get to choose when to leave,* she says. She's still sitting down. We're both bad at goodbyes. The song hasn't finished.

She says: *I need to see a man about a dog.*

In our bubble, we didn't have a song. We had dozens. Hundreds. A song for every mood, every memory. Songs we sang while drunk. Songs we played in the time between sex and sleep. Songs we sent each other in the middle of the night because, *You really need to hear this.*

In our bubble, a thing we did is make each other playlists. It wasn't about the songs as much as it was the titles. Our playlists had names like *4am Post-Whiskey Drinking Pre-Hangover Bed-Bound Blues. Minstrels For Menstruals. Emo Brunch. Sketches for My Sweetheart the Punk.*

You could come with me, she says. *Help me leave.* The song finishes. I can feel her eyes on me. *But you're my memory*, I say. *Don't I get to decide when you go.* The speakers play a looping static, the sound you get when a side ends. *You haven't changed,* she says. *You know, I tried. I wanted to give you a chance to do the right thing. I shouldn't have bothered.* She leaves. I let her.

The mountains outside flatline as the carriage door closes.

An announcement says she never loved me.

Liar, I say. No one is listening.

Nine

Colorado / Obsession, Part II

The sway of the carriage is hypnotic, metronomic. The click of the wheels on the track claps steady against the hum of the engine, a diesel electric boombox burrowing deep into the mountain. An occasional low grumble suggests the train is not a morning person either.

Jon is still snoozing. I sit down opposite, place a mostly cold cup of train coffee in front of him. He opens one eye. *Howdy, pilgrim,* he says, and then, *you shouldn't have.* He takes his flask out, tops up the coffee with whatever paint thinner he last filled it with.

She gone, he says. I nod and tell him she just needed time to think. *For the best,* he says. *We got a broken boy to fix, and we're two days down.* He takes a sip of hooch coffee. *Is there anything else I need to know,* I say. He thinks about it a moment, counts on his fingers. *Let's see, New York, the end. Yadda Yadda.* He looks up. *Oh, the key. We'll need that.* I ask what key. He shrugs. *It's your head, champ. You'll figure it out.*

A thing I do sometimes is talk to my dog. His name is Fisher. Technically he doesn't exist, being imaginary and all, but that doesn't stop him taking walks with me. Or following commands. *Sit. Siiiiit. Good boy.* He walks by my heel and wags his tail and pants and is an absolute joy.

That thing you read about dogs being the key to happiness.

I'm thirteen, sitting on my bike at the top of a set of steps near my house. There are eight. I'm trying to find the courage to ride down them. I've sat here for hours, too scared to do it. My brother has done it. Paul has done it. *Fuck it*, I say, and go. It's easier than I ever imagined.

The mountains – slate grey, snow-capped – look like the Rockies, but not just the Rockies. The hills of my childhood are here too. Lesser peaks of the Lake District, limestone pavement of the Yorkshire Dales. A slope behind our house that my brother and I used to sledge down.

He tosses me my notebook. *You write today, champ.* I roll it up, hold it in both hands. *I'll write tomorrow*, I say. He stands in the aisle, stretches. *Well, you know what they say*, he says, holding the ends of his feet. *Women weaken words.*

Announcement: *Remember when she said she just wanted to work on herself for a while.*

When Sophia broke up with me, I couldn't concentrate, couldn't work, couldn't read. Couldn't write. A week later, I quit my job. Figured I'd find something else. I didn't. Life is consequences.

The way I quit my job was by dumping my laptop on my manager's desk, saying, *I'm done*, and walking out. HR tried to call, but I turned off my phone. I also changed the Twitter password and the recovery email address. Before I left I scheduled a few final tweets.

Sample tweet: *Protects everything but your reputation. Bye JoeSeal.*

Sample tweet: *Load up on guns and kill your fence. Bye JoeSeal.*

Sample tweet: *Don't judge a tin by its Twitter. Bye JoeSeal.*

BASE Fatality #5 is Pauli Belik. Between jumps his pack got wet and froze during transit. By the time Pauli jumped from the Kaknäs tower in Stockholm, his canopy was encased in ice and didn't inflate. He died on impact with the floor. It was 7 March 1983. I was five days old.

Jon is hopped up on coffee. I ask him the plan. *We deadhead this wagon to the next stop*, he says, *at which point we try and gank a whip to the end of the line, see if we can't find the key and flip the doohickey that fixes you.* He slaps my shoulder and I nod like I understand.

The track has levelled off. The train lurches underfoot. We clutch at headrests to brace ourselves. Jon looks out of the window. A churn of cedars wash past. *She's pulling too fast*, he says. *The highball on one of these engines is a buck-fifty. We must be pushing a buck-seventy, seventy-five.*

Say what you want about Jon Bon Jovi, he knows his trains.

We skip through the carriages at full clip, each filled with faces and bodies I've known, all my past crushes, sitting in seats, talking among themselves. My barista, a girl from my gym. A popular blogger. A woman I saw on the bus the other day. They don't notice me.

I realise I've stopped running. Jon takes my arm. I ask him if this is about obsession. *It's about addiction,* he says. *But these are crushes,* I say. *I wasn't addicted to them all.* The carriage doors slide open. *I meant collectively,* Jon says. *You're addicted to women.*

We push through another two carriages before we arrive at a door we can't open. A keypad sits square in the middle of the door. Jon punches a few numbers. A series of red LEDs flash above the keypad. He slaps the door with an open palm. *Dammit.* I ask what he tried. *My birthday, obviously.* The door is cold rolled steel, no seams, no rivets. It has no business being here. I tell him to try my birthday, if he even knows it. *Of course I know it,* he says, *you just write it funny.*

Through a window I can see the engine as we curve around a bend, the livery gleaming white like an unpainted model train. We're a few cars back. Below, a mountain meadow hosts a crop of her hair. The strands, glossy, golden, shimmer in the breeze. Jon punches my birthday. The LEDs flash green. The door swings out towards us to reveal iron bars, a cage door without a key. Jon grips a bar with each fist. *Got a plan there, chief.*

I was thirteen when I first learned Jon and I share a birthday: 2 March.

A thing people never say: *Talking to your imaginary dog is the first sign of madness.*

An idea. *What would Jon Voigt do,* I say. Like most people, Jon is a fan of the 1985 classic *Runaway Train*, in which Jon Voigt uncouples the engine, saves the day, dies a hero. Spoiler alert. I'm suggesting the uncoupling part, not the blaze nor indeed the glory. *No good,* Jon says. *She's got a helper, mid-train.* I wait for him to explain. *A second engine helps the main one push up steep grades,* Jon says. *We have to get behind it. Or you could just unlock this gate.* I tell him I don't have the key. *I believe you,* he says, as if it were in question.

There was nothing more erotic than her hip bone. The pale softness off it. The jutting angular form of it. In our bubble I'm biting her hip, kissing it, gripping it with my free hand as we fuck.

Announcement: *Remember when she stopped texting back.*

Beyond the iron gate, the door to the next carriage swings open and we find ourselves face-to-shifting-face with him, the Many-Faced Man, separated only by iron. It looks like he's smirking, all of his faces pulling the same satisfied grin. He takes a key from his pocket, steps forward, lifts it to the lock. I ask Jon who that is. *Let's not stick around to find out,* he says.

The carriages have shifted. Memory is impermanent. Inconvenient. The train worms its way through a series of tunnels in the mountain rock, each time changing the setting around us. Outside, snow-wrapped mountains flicker like torches as we race past. For minutes at a time the train is wrapped in a cloak of black. We run in the shade.

Cut to a gym car filled with several versions of me, honing their already well-conditioned physiques. The walls of mirrors make them look infinitely better, me much worse. Their muscles, taut, tanned, were once mine. Old priorities, fresh anxieties. They watch me walk, heckling my body. Jon turns back to me. *You used to be a real dick.*

Darkness.

Cut to a carriage piled with newspapers and pizza boxes and trash, and a voice telling me I'm a slob. Cut to a carriage where I'm masturbating to memories of Sophia months after she ended us. Each a scene from the lives I've lived. Each an addiction. The train speeds up. One-eighty. One-ninety. We climb along the aisle using headrests for traction. *Hold on,* Jon says. *We're nearly there. You've got this.* But I haven't.

Cut to a carriage where I'm in bed, unable to shower or shave or eat or get dressed or do anything but stare blankly at my phone because a depressive state is addictive too and once you're down and prone to wallow without energy to try it's so tempting to let yourself slip further from any semblance of humanity until you're convinced you deserved this and she's better off without you. Darkness.

Our first conversation was all wide eyes, long takes. We shared cigarettes between bands, laughed, teased, looked. I was nicotine high, drunk on bourbon and promise. It was a dance, really. The kind of conversation where the subtext is *I want you in my mouth.*

Over the loudspeaker, her voice: *I'm sorry, I'm sorry, I'm sorry.* It repeats on a loop. What she's sorry for is breaking my heart. It's what she kept saying when it ended. *I'm sorry.* It was the answer to every question. *I'm sorry.* It echoes in my head. *I'm sorry.*

I say: *Why do you think I'm addicted to women.*
He says: *Why do you think that you're not.*
I say: *My dick doesn't work any more.*
He says: *That's not entirely true.*

We're between carriages when he turns, offers me a drink. I decline. He takes a swig, says something, but the cladding on the car is thin and I can hear only the train. I nod along. He gives me a pat on the shoulder, strides into the next carriage. I caught none of it. Everything was vestibule and nothing heard.

Voices behind us now. We race into the next carriage, barricade the door with our bodies. *One more*, Jon says. He reaches for the kind of pipe that's always lying around in these situations, slides it through the handle, barring the door. I stand to find myself an inch away from the Many-Faced Man, our noses separated by glass. His features, unmoored, random, shift in the strobing light of the vestibule. He's flanked by more bodies, by my wrongs. They're shouting, angry. He reaches for the door handle, wrenching it. Jon pulls me towards the other end of the car.

We open the door, stop. The back carriage is already uncoupled. Sophia stands in the doorway, drifting away from us. Over the loudspeaker, a record skipping: *I'm sorry.* Behind her a handsome Golden Retriever pants happily. Fisher. She's got my dog. *I'm sorry.*

Fisher's tail wags hard, clips the edge of a metal rack. Drops of blood spatter the wall. Happy tail. She looks at him, then at me. *I'm sorry.* My heart is tied to her carriage by an invisible thread. The door slams shut and rips it from my chest like a loose tooth. *I'm sorry.*

In our bubble we're arguing. She grabs her bag, heads for the door. *Don't go*, I say. She leaves. I get a text a few minutes later. *Was that supposed to make me stay*, she says. *At least say it like you mean it.* I run after her but it's too late. She's gone. I text back. *I meant it*, I say. *Really.*

BASE Fatality #74 is Bill Frogge. On 27 January 2003, during a jump in Utah, Bill deployed his pilot chute, only for it to pull free. He fell to the desert floor, died on impact. The knot securing the chute to the main canopy was never tied. There was no inquest. He prepared his own rig.

Is it still suicide if you drop the catch.

I clutch at my chest, somehow still intact. *What does she need Fisher for,* I say. Jon is pacing, thinking. *I know that hurt,* he says, *but this mustang's still running and we don't have any reins.* Behind us, my wrongs beat at the carriage door. Jon opens the side of the car, licks a finger, raises it to the wind. *Bad news: we're pulling two-hundred.* He grabs a handle, hangs out of the door. *Worse news, there's a curve ahead we won't make at this speed.* I stick my head out, see a bridge swerving away from us over a mountain lake. *We have to jump,* he says. We peer down at the lake. *If I die in here,* I say. He interrupts. *No time.* He takes my hand. We jump on three.

If we were wearing chutes, this would count as a Span jump. Span is the S in BASE. A bridge is a span. But this isn't a BASE jump. We're not wearing chutes. There's nothing to catch us.

The fall sucks the air from my lungs. Every nerve ending fires at once. My stomach somersaults. Something beats where my heart used to be. Time moves at half speed. We're still falling. There's nothing to catch us. It's not suicide if you're trying to save your life.

We hit the water hard and keep falling. We float, dazed, confused. Suspended and embryonic in the freezing lake.

I feel Jon kick and do the same. We surface, still holding hands, expecting explosions, fireworks. But there is no crash, no wreckage.

The train navigated the curve without incident, marched on without us. *Huh,* Jon says. He grins at me like the sheriff who shot the shark. *I always wanted to do that.*

I punch the water, play-acting. He looks worried. *Fuck,* I say. *Lost my train of thought.*

Jon laughs so hard he almost drowns.

Ten

Nebraska / Greed

We're halfway up a river we've never heard of in a boat we don't own when the storm begins in earnest. The skies open with great rips, tin foil clouds being torn apart by their own fury. Our boat has a bum fuel gauge and a leaky hull, a pebble making ripples in a puddle. Jon sticks his head out of the cab. *Strap in, chief,* he says. *No time to find a bigger boat.*

I'm sitting at the stern, sullen, watching Jon sing. He's having the time of his life, belting sea shanties, making short work of a rum stash he found below deck. He's a great entertainer, even if you're not in the mood to be entertained. He swigs rum, shouts over his shoulder. *What I've been wondering is this,* he says. *Is it still a road trip if you're nowhere near a road.*

That thing you read about love having the same effect on the brain as cocaine.

Would you have let her go, he says.
I might have, I say. *I don't know.*
Then why say that you would.
Because I want her to stay.

I still dream about her. Sometimes we meet for the first time and flirt. Sometimes we undress each other and kiss. I always wake as we're about to fuck. Sometimes I'm watching her flirt with someone else. Those aren't the worst dreams. The worst dreams are the ones where we're happy.

I'm six, playing in the sea with my brother, swimming in inflatable rings. The tide carries us out further than we realise. Mum runs to the sea, stands up to her knees, calls to us. It looks like she's waving. We wave back, laugh like it's a game. It isn't. She starts shouting. We kick harder, and she walks out to meet us. When we reach her, she hugs us both tight. *Don't ever do that to me again,* she says. She's crying. We start crying too. *We didn't mean to,* I say. She lets go and looks at me. *It's okay now,* she says, shaking. *I just needed you to swim back before you drifted away.*

I'm thirteen, on a family holiday in France. I read that a girl drowned in a nearby lake. It was a public holiday, and the lake was crowded with families. Hundreds of people watched the girl drown assuming someone else would help. By the time someone jumped in, it was too late.

That's how I felt much of the time, like I was sinking, and no one would jump in to help.

I guess it's hard to tell if someone is drowning when they're on dry land.

Jon is nine verses into a shanty he wrote when the engine quits. We're adrift on a raft we can't steer in a river we can't see. He starts hitting things with a spanner. The water runs rough beneath us. I can make out the firs of submerged trees before they disappear into fog. Maybe this is where addiction gets you, floating aimlessly down a river of your own poor judgement.

Twice now I've watched Sophia leave and done nothing.

I'm thirty, at a gig in Camden. The first time I see her she's standing in the middle of the room, swaying, burning, casually oblivious to the world orbiting around her. The band are terrible. Not that I'm listening. She smiles and suddenly nothing else matters. When we lock eyes I'm already lost. Man down. As we move towards each other, colour drains from everything but her. Later we'll learn we both work in music, her for a label; me, a magazine. But now I lean close, say something I don't remember, something she doesn't hear. It doesn't matter. We don't need words.

We stand by the bar, achingly close. She's wearing a leather jacket over a dress. I'm wearing black jeans, nerves. I'm staring at her lips, trying not to shake. Her head is tilted towards me, her mouth open a touch. We hold still, each daring the other to make a move. She grabs my collar, pulls me towards her. Lips meet, then bodies. She tastes of wine, cigarettes. She presses against me, gets me hard. I can feel her pubic bone through her dress. As we part, I utter a single *fuck*. I raise my fingers to my lips, find traces of her there. She smiles and the world grows distant.

The ship has turned sideways in the current. Jon is leaning into the engine bay, cursing. I'm thinking about her. I feel sick. That sunken stomach you get when your heart breaks, when an addict goes cold turkey. I rush out to the stern, lean over the side, loose my guts into the water.

I'm thirty-one, sitting at my desk when the text arrives, the one that says she's ending it. I run to the bathroom, drop to my knees, eject vomit and tears and mucus. From the floor of the toilet I manage a one-word reply: *Why*. I curse at myself for sending it so soon.

Boats, heartbreak: I don't have the stomach for either.

I'm watching the bile slick I just formed float away when I notice the propeller is snagged on something. *Skipper, looks like we're caught up.* Jon sticks his head up from the engine bay and raises high his wrench. *We'll make a sailor of you yet, lad,* he says.

I hold his legs while he reaches down to grab whatever we've hooked. A few seconds later I'm hit square in the face with a bundle of sodden fabric. *Here's your culprit,* Jon says. I unroll the shredded cloth. It's a dress. One of Sophia's. I toss it down to the deck, lean over the side, dunk my arm into the sound. I hold fast a second, then feel something brush my fingertips. I pull it into the boat. Another dress. I fish again, pull up a pair of lace knickers I bought her, part of a set.

A few minutes of fishing later and my haul includes pyjamas, socks, some band T-shirts I gave her, stockings, summer dresses, more lingerie. We sway with the roll of the hull, sizing up our haul. Jon holds up a bra: black, lacy. *Your girlfriend isn't even here and she's holding us back.*

Girlfriend. Jon looks sorry as soon as he says it. The word glows neon, hangs overhead, floating through the fog until it's just a blur of green light.

In our bubble we've just got home from a gig. We strip, too drunk to fool around but we fumble and paw anyway. Her phone beeps, lights up. It's well after one. I ask who it is and she says, *It doesn't matter,* and I say something like, *Maybe you should sleep at his.* Tears then as she slumps to the bed, crushed under the twin weight of jealousy and fatigue. *I can't do this any more.*

She isn't my girlfriend, I say. Jon apologises. The thing about words is that they can't be unsaid.

Rain drives through the zipper of the mackintosh I'm wearing, the kind fishermen have. I don't know who it belongs to. We leave our catch and seek shelter in the cabin. I de-mack, slump to my seat. Jon tries the engine. It labours, turns over. *I'm gonna raise the prop,* he says. *Won't be as fast but should keep us clear of debris.* I stare at the floor. He waits for words that don't arrive, lets my silence drown in the sound of the engine.

Four words repeat in my head: *I. Can't. Do. This.*

In our bubble we've collapsed to the floor in laughing fits because an intern at her office only just discovered Jeff Buckley drowned in 1995. She came in dressed in black, sobbing. Sophia shows me her Instagram tribute: *Can't believe it. So young. So sad. RIP Jeff.* Later, we'll punctuate silences, inappropriate moments, with a solemn *RIP Jeff* and crack up all over again.

In our bubble we fell fast, intertwined, codependent, spun together in an earthbound spiral. We tumbled through vinyl afternoons, latex mornings. We spent days in bed, pushed everything else away. Flaked on friends. Fixed cocktails, cancelled plans. I skipped work, skipped therapy. We were insatiable, intoxicated. We lost perspective. There was nothing keeping us afloat. I couldn't stop. I didn't want to. I fell further, faster. Too far. I didn't care. *You make me feel so good.* It grew fragile, precarious. I wanted more. Lust crazed, love sick. Lost. She bailed. She had to. Pulled the cord before she hit the floor. Landed on solid ground. *I can't do this any more.*

It's not suicide if you catch yourself.

I'm still falling.

Over the sound of the pistons, a quiet song. Jon is singing to himself. It's not a shanty. It's one of his, one of my favourites. I quietly sing the lines with him. Lyrics my lips haven't said in a long time. They remember. This song was my first of his. Tears well in my eyes as he hits the chorus. I think about Sophia. About how much she hates Jon's music, his band. I laugh. It's not a loud laugh. It doesn't last long. But it tempers the tears. Tames them. I taste salt between my lips, let them fall open. I join Jon on the second verse, softly at first, slowly letting my lungs fill, until I take a deep breath and sing with everything I have. He leaves the wheel, sits with me. We sing, his arm over my shoulders, trembling as I choke back tears. We sing as hard as we know how. For us. Because it feels good. Every goddamn line. Even the storm quiets to hear us.

The boat sits low in the river. Jon is slouching over the wheel, tilting to one side. It's hard to tell who is steering who. *Maybe we got lost in the fog,* I say. *Nonsense,* he says. *River only goes two ways. Way we came, and the way we're going.* It's hard to argue with his logic. *I can't figure anything in this fog,* I say. He laughs. *What's to figure,* he says. *The fog is the thing.*

I'm thirty-one and she's breaking my heart. Her text is simple: *I can't do this any more.* I loose a single word as I read it: *Fuck.* This is how the bubble bursts, not with a bang but a whisper.

I reach to my back pocket. *Fuck*, I say. My notebook is still on the train.

If you can only see one cloud, you might be in the middle of it.

Eleven

Nebraska / Greed, Part II

Shapes and shadows move in the mist, all faded silhouettes, faint whispers. In a silent pantomime I see my brother and me riding through the woods on bikes. My brother and me playing with Tomorrow Knights. My brother and me climbing trees. Through a clearing I see us on the river bank. We must be eight, nine, dressed like unspecific superheroes.

Across the river, Sophia and I stand either side of a toddler, helping her walk. Our daughter. Sophia smiles at me. I'm dressed the way I always thought I might someday: cotton shirt. A blazer. The kind of shoes people admire. She's in a dress, a Burberry coat. We look so happy. I close my eyes, keep them shut tight, the way kids do when they pretend to be invisible.

Hope is the cruellest emotion.

You wanted that, Jon says. *Kids.* I nod. *Never made sense before,* I say. *But with her, I could see it.* Jon doesn't reply. He watches my eyes drop lower until I'm staring at the floor. *Sometimes I dream about her pregnant. Sometimes we're at the hospital, being handed our baby for the first time. Sometimes we're out for a walk, holding her hands.* He approaches several sentences, swallows them. Finally he changes the subject: *How come you never talk about your brother.*

I'm seven, my brother is eight, we're racing our bikes through the woods. He keeps racing ahead, telling me I'm slow. Frustrated, I crash into him on purpose. I don't realise that part of my pedal is broken, that the metal sticking out is sharp. It tears a chunk of flesh out of his leg. I wrap my T-shirt around it and help him hobble home. He needs seven stitches. He doesn't talk to me for weeks.

I'm thirteen and my brother is fourteen, we're on holiday with our parents. There's a girl at the resort I like. He hooks up with her right in front of me. I don't leave my room for two days. We tore chunks out of each other growing up, physical, emotional. They were always forgiven.

But then, there were always more chunks to tear.

I say: *I talk about my brother all the time.*
Jon says: *No, champ, you barely mention him.*

The river swells, swallows the tree line, kicks up silt that swirls muddy brown in our wake. An orchestra of raindrops play a coda on the cabin roof. What I love about rain is it has substance, atmosphere. There's something arrogant about the sun. Something smug. Rain is relatable.

It must be mid-afternoon. Jon is soberish, skippering with all his heart. We're floating above a highway now, the lamp posts rising from the sound a dead giveaway. Their swan necks crane over the surface, glow bright in the gloom. A road trip in a boat is still a road trip after all.

Jon says: *When was the last time you saw your therapist.*

When my brother and I weren't playing Tomorrow Knights,

we made up our own heroes. We'd tie towels round our necks, slip underpants over our trousers. My superpowers were on the abstract end: being able to look at my watch as the second hand passed the 12. Appearing to be sound asleep when our parents came to tuck us in. Running really fast whenever I wore my red trainers. Most people want to be able to fly. Not me. My favourite heroes couldn't fly. They had wires, webs, retractable wings. They had to figure out ways to catch themselves.

The call is faint at first. *Hello.* A voice in the fog. *Is anyone there.* Up ahead, port side, a hazy silhouette that slowly sharpens into focus. A woman, standing on a jetty. Jon manoeuvres us alongside, I jump out with a rope. The jetty is a mostly submerged truck, sitting perpendicular to the river. I tie off the rope on an upright exhaust. The woman steps forward, smiles. My therapist. Dr Young. Emily. It's never particularly surprising to see people you know wandering around your own mind, but the moments they choose to appear can sometimes feel a little on the nose.

Haven't see you in a while. I ask her how long it's been. I'm supposed to see her every week. I've lost track. *A month, maybe. Six weeks. Too long.* We sit down. *I should have come to see you.* She smiles politely, asks how I've been. *Things have been a little unusual,* I say, nodding towards Jon. He's sitting at the wheel, singing sea shanties, replacing all maritime references with the word river. *I can see that.* she says. *We've got an hour. What's on your mind.*

The way you remember which is port side is this: left and port have four letters.

Other four letter words: Love. Hope. Stay. Don't. Fuck.

Emily and I have been seeing each other for a year, meeting

a couple of times a month. She's not my first therapist. I had another, before. Stopped seeing her when I met Sophia. In our bubble my brain was mostly bearable. I swapped self-care for Sophia and thought everything would be okay.

I'm thirty-one, going cold turkey off my meds, drinking wine, sobbing into yesterday's T-shirt. Suddenly stopping a course of antidepressants is strongly discouraged. So is excessive drinking. It says so on the pamphlet in the box, but I didn't check. I'm not big on instructions.

Cymbalta. 30mg. If you stop taking this shit without tapering off, side effects may include: suicidal tendencies, uncontrollable crying, and a sudden desire to listen to eighties power ballads.

First thing Emily did was ask me to build a safe space, a place in my mind I could retreat to when things were stressful. Somewhere that would calm me down. I imagined a forest, described the scene to her. I said I'd been there once, that I'd seen redwoods. It didn't matter that I hadn't.

Emily is making notes as I speak, but her eyes never leave me for long. She's in her forties, slight, sharp-featured, smartly dressed. The word that best describes her is warm. If she wasn't a therapist, she might be a primary school teacher. Sometimes, when I get particularly sad, tears well in her eyes. What she does is takes whatever is upsetting me and offers ways to help deal with it.

Less a therapist, more a pain whisperer.

It doesn't sound like you're being very kind to yourself, she says. Jon laughs, tells her about the billboards, my Technicolor torso forty feet high. She asks if that's true. *I don't get to decide those things*, I say. *They just are.* The look I give Jon is brine and chum. He waves himself away. *Of course you get to decide*, she says. I see my reflection in the water. Rippled, distorted. *She doesn't want me any more*, I say. Emily gives me a look that says we've been over this. *You think if you looked different*, she says, *she'd come back.* I nod. *She might.* Emily asks what I looked liked when we were together. I say I looked the same. *And she was attracted to you then.* I kick at the anchor. I'm being defeated by rational thought. It doesn't feel good.

My superpower is taking myself too seriously.

In our bubble I'm feeling shy about my body. Sophia tells me I'm silly. She slips my T-shirt over my head, pulls down my boxers, kisses me everywhere. She takes her time, her breath hot, lips wet. Finally, she drapes her hair over my hard-on, tickling, teasing, until I feel the warm envelope of her mouth wrap over the head. Still going slow, she pulls the hair from her face so I can watch. I feel her tongue trace the length of my cock, base to tip. *See*, she says, *I love your body.*

Emily says everyone has three versions of themselves. There's the side we show to other people. She calls this our best self. Then there's our inner child. That's where all our joy and curiosity comes from. But the inner child is vulnerable to the third side, our bully. She says it's the job of the best self to protect the child from the bully.

She says: *What would you say if someone spoke about Jon like that.* I say: *I'd tell them to fuck off.*

She asks about the overdose, if it was accident or intention. *Depends if I survive*, I say. I laugh. It falls quiet. *Just because it ended,* Emily says, *doesn't mean it wasn't good.* I nod like I didn't need to hear that. *We were good.* I say. I take a deep breath. *Then suddenly we weren't any more.* She's listening so intently it makes my voice wobble. Tears well in her eyes. We stay like that a moment. Then she looks at her watch. Our time is up. We say our goodbyes. She walks down the dock, disappears into a bank of fog. Hours are always doing that to you, ending.

You feel any better, Jon says. I untie the dock line, throw it into the boat. *What is it about someone listening to you for an hour,* I say. Jon pulls me aboard. *Maybe it's because you finally get to talk about yourself,* he says. *You never do that.* I mouth the words *fuck off* and he laughs.

The fog lifts like a skirt, leaving us naked, exposed. The water looks black. *Company,* Jon says. I stand to see the riverbanks lined with memories. My wrongs. He's with them. The guy with his face in perma-flux.

He raises his hand and the assembled army brace themselves for something. We flinch as he drops his arm. What they throw is words. *Nobody likes you. You're a terrible person. You don't matter.* Jon and I relax some. This isn't so bad. Then the Many-Faced Man throws his head back, laughs. A booming laugh. They're all laughing now. Doubled over, leaning on each other. Pointing at me. I'm shouting: *Fuck off. Fuck off. Fuck off.* Still they laugh. I can't quiet them all.

I don't know how to turn it off. Jon grabs me by both shoulders, tells me to ignore them. My face makes a half-grin grimace. The kind of expression I imagine looks like I forgot how to have a face. *Come on, chief, I need your help inside.* He pulls me into the cabin, bolts the door. *Don't worry*, he says. *I've got this*. He throws the throttle forward. The pistons race from hum to growl.

And then, nothing. We're not going any faster. *Well shit, that was disappointing*. He tells me to take the wheel. *You got this*, he says. *You're in control*. I keep the nose of the boat pointed at the horizon, grip the wheel so tight the vibrations of the motor course through me like fury.

When I let myself look, the banks of the river are fir-lined, memory free. I'm about to thank Jon when the first stone sails through the window, narrowly missing my face. More rocks rain on the roof, leaving large dents, shattering the windows. We duck for cover. *I preferred the laughter*, I say. Something large, likely a rock, hits the console. The engine dies. Jon disagrees. *You know what they say*, he says. *Sticks and stones will break your boat, but names will never leave you.*

The stoning is blissfully finite. We start to drift downstream. I thank Jon for steering me through the storm. *Hey*, he says. *I'm your Huckleberry.*

I'm thirty-two, post bubble, handing over her things. I don't have much. A pair of socks, some toiletries, couple of books. I could have met her somewhere, could have bagged it up, brought it all with me. I didn't. I made her come to my flat. What I hoped would happen was she'd kiss me. One more time. With feeling. She doesn't. What she does is takes her things and leaves.

Here's what she said to me as she left: *It never would have lasted.*

My superpower is remembering.

Twelve

Iowa / Anger

The highway's littered with abandoned cars left lying at odd angles. As if they'd swerved to a stop all at once. Some sit empty with doors open, others filled with things. Belongings, junk. Both. We check each for keys as we hike. It's been an hour since we left the boat, an hour of hot road, heat stroke. Everything is tired feet and tension. It's sunset on day two. We need a car.

I call out to Jon: *You wanna explain this.*
Nah, he says. *What's to explain.*
Why are they running.
They're scared.
Of what.
Of you.

I'm six, walking the dog in the woods with my nana and brother. We arrive at a white wall of fog. It cuts our path as far as we can see in either direction. Thick, sat flush against an invisible face. No glass, no screen. Smoke frozen solid. A barrier between here and beyond. The dog is barking. I want to touch it. Nana tells us to turn around and we leave.

I'm fifteen, watching an episode of *The X-Files* with my dad. Mum is in hospital for an operation on her back. The episode is about people being mutilated in a hospital ward. During an ad break he looks over to see that I'm sitting, petrified, tears in my eyes, and tells me not to worry about Mum. He says we should turn it off, watch something else. *I'm okay,* I say. *Leave it on.* I need to see Mulder and Scully save the day before I sleep.

The sun is falling, singeing the clouds. *What's happening,* I say. Jon doesn't answer right away. *Short version or long version,* he says. I don't wait for his answer. *I'm dying, aren't I.* He mumbles something about how we're all dying. I tell him maybe we should have helped Sophia. *Maybe you're delirious,* he says. I check a sun visor for keys, come up empty. *What if it was the right thing to do.* He wipes tired eyes. *The right thing to do is to look after yourself.* I slam a car door hard enough to shatter the window. *What do you care, really,* I say. He curses, kicks a Chevy. *I'm just the guy who's always been here,* he says. *The guy who isn't trying to leave. You're right, I don't know shit. Like I don't know you don't listen to my music any more.*

Jon's flaw is he needs to be needed. His fear is irrelevance.

I say: *She has the key.*
He says: *You sure.*

A ball of flame blazes overhead. A missile, a mortar. A meteor. It burns out, drops into a nearby lake bed. I look up to see more streaking through the sky, red clouds raining fire.

I saw one once, a meteorite. I was twenty-four. It was big, searing across the sky. A jet engine, free of its mooring, fast and wrapped in flame. It scorched the air for a few hundred yards above my house before I lost it behind a treeline. I asked around for days after, checked the news. Nothing. Later I realised what it was. What it must have been.

Is it still a shooting star if it falls to earth, or is it just a rock.

Remember to get the sound in your damn book. Somewhere in the dusk light a dog is barking. The horizon carries the high-pitched hum of a motorbike. Nearby, a car door slams. Closer still, my heart beating between my ears. Sound is very important.

On the wind a whisper: *Fuck. Fuck. Fuck.*

It's funny how you frame things when you don't know the answers. When I was a teenager I'd get headaches, almost daily. My first thought was cancer. Second was meningitis. Something bad. It had to be. I stopped taking painkillers. I thought drugs would make the cancer-gitis worse. Or work to weaken my immune system.

Later, rationale took over. Maybe a weird-looking fog was just fog. Maybe stars raining from the sky were just bits of dust and rock. Maybe a break-up was just a break-up.

That thing you read about men being chronically dehydrated.

We summit a slight crest in the road. The kind of crest that would make your stomach capsize if you took it by car. It capsizes anyway. I see her hair first. A finite golden braid. She's under the hood of a Cadillac convertible, shouting. *Fuck, fuck, fuck.*

She sees me, falls silent. My feet are stuck. My words too. I'm sweating. She drops the hood, stands, hands on hips. Synapses fire. Nerves flash and smoulder like spent matches. Surprise, outrage, lust, anger, joy. A hundred wires tangled in my chest like headphones in a coat pocket.

It's no accident that the heart is halfway between the dick and brain.

He says: *Now you've done it.*
I say: *What the fuck is your problem.*
He says: *I can't help you if you won't help you.*

In 1979, NASA's Skylab fell out of orbit and plummeted to Earth, scattering debris across Western Australia, burning bits of metal flaring in the sky like fireworks. Luckily, no property was hit and no one injured, though one district fined NASA $500 for littering. They never paid.

The setting sun behind us gives everything a glow. Golden hour. Jon and I walk towards her. She wipes her hands on a T-shirt that used to be white, glares at me, her expression salt and citrus.

They say that white isn't a colour at all, that it's all the colours at once. Maybe love is like that. Not one emotion, but all of them.

Coincidence is a cliché.
But this isn't a coincidence.
What the fuck are you on about.
You wanted her to be here, he says.
I'm not gonna miss your cryptic bullshit.
He grins at me. *Hooper drives the boat, chief.*

We're close enough to speak now. *What the fuck.* She's pissed. She blames me for engine trouble. For not letting her go. It's not that I'm not listening, but as she started her speech I was accosted by a handsome golden retriever. I pat his ribs, let him lick my hands, stop him jumping up. Bad for the hips. *You and me are fighting, buddy.*

Sophia is waiting for me to acknowledge her. I do. *I've been on a river cruise*, I say. *How the hell would I know about your goddamn engine.* She mutters something I don't hear. Jon is writing in the dirt on the back windscreen of an abandoned car: *This too shall come out in the wash.*

I say: *Stop being such a cheese toastie.*
She says: *Stop being such a cunt.*

Motorbikes. The hum and wail of two-stroke engines drifts from background to foreground, revs cracking in the air. Overpowered lawnmowers. I was too busy listening to the bass line in my chest. Missed the drop. Can't see them yet. There must be dozens. A gang, a pack. I ask Jon if this is bad. *It isn't good*, he says. Sophia is back in the driver's seat turning the key, pumping the gas. *Come on, come on, come on.*

Over the crest I see a face that isn't. Paul. He holds his hand up to wave. A greeting, a taunt. I don't know. Then them. Mistakes. Accidents. Hints and allegations. Grey clouds loom above. Riders on the storm, cloaked in black. An army. Then their leader, the Many-Faced Man. He waves too. This wave is meant as a taunt. One that says, *We're coming.*

Who is that, Sophia says.
You don't know.
Should I.

The road between us is shrinking. I tell Sophia to try the engine. She shouts back. *It doesn't work.* I reach over, grab the keys, twist them in the ignition. The engine turns over. *You're fucking kidding*, she says. I get in back, call Fisher. Jon is fifty yards away. He hops into the cab of an abandoned gas tanker, the kind that tends to be lying around in these situations. The engine fires for him first try. He swings the steering wheel, shouts at us through the window. *Go, go, go.*

There is a highway in my mind littered with cars. Sophia weaves between them, pedal floored. In the back seat, Fisher rests his chin on my thigh. *It's okay, boy*, I say. Behind us, Jon is having the time of his life. He dances the tanker over the road, grinning like ol' Jack Burton, clipping cars, crushing others. In his wake a dozen memories knocked from their bikes.

Still they come. I've made enemies of my own memories. Refugees of others. Perhaps they're ones that don't fit the narrative any more. Perhaps I keep changing the narrative. It's hard to keep the story straight when you don't know what you're doing.

A bridge. Jon is singing to himself. One of his. He gives me the thumbs up and throws the steering wheel to the right and then all the way to the left. The trailer jackknifes, swinging out to the side as he hits the bridge. The whole thing tips over and skids towards us, screeching, sparks flying. It comes to a rest halfway across, blocking the entire road.

Sophia slams on the brakes. The cab opens, Jon hops down. The sound of splashing liquid, the smell of petrol. He takes a match he's been chewing, lights it on the sole of his boot, tosses it to the floor. Flame crosses the road behind him and engulfs the tanker.

He jumps in the passenger seat and looks at Sophia. *Whenever you're ready.* The wail of tyres, the smell of sweat. Behind us, the kind of explosion you might expect from a fully laden gas tanker taking out a bridge. *Should slow them down,* Jon says. It's the coolest thing I've ever seen.

Jon says: *Nice moves, hot shot.*
She says: *Not so bad yourself.*
Jon says: *It was all his idea.*

The bonfire is a dot in the distance by the time the sun sets. Fireflies dance in the corn fields. Black clouds roll in from the edge of the sky. The air is charged with storm static. We stop to close the roof. Golden hour is over, replaced by the twilight haze of dusk.

Hours are always doing that to you, ending.

I was never allowed to ride motorbikes. One of my uncles died in a motorbike accident. My other uncle messed up his knees and hips coming off one. My dad rode motorbikes. But my brother and I couldn't. One of those dad rules. *I rode motorbikes so you don't have to.* I wouldn't get on one now, is the thing. Far too dangerous. My father's fear is my fear.

She kept saying I didn't know her, not really. Maybe I didn't. All I knew was what she told me. What she let me see. We're all fictions.

Sophia's deal is she wants to be liked. She shows you things that make you like her. Her fear is showing you anything that might persuade you otherwise.

On the side of the road we pass a woman walking, her back to us. Her hair is long, straight, dark. She's strolling under the lights on the hard shoulder. As we pass, I turn to see her face, only when I look she's walking in the opposite direction, her back to me. I never saw her turn around.

Friend of yours, Jon says.
Kind of, I say. *That was my ex-wife.*

The road east rolls unrelenting through fields, national parks. The hours tick over with the miles. It's late when I realise I've lost time, lying prostrate on the back seat. I passed out at some point, fatigued, fevered. I sit in a half sleep, reality shifting like the slides in a View-Master.

The storm has drawn closer and the clouds, like vast lanterns, are strobing red. I'm sweating, even though it's night, even though it's still twenty-two degrees. Jon is driving now. He turns to look at me. *You doing okay.* I mumble something about being fine. The truth of it is I don't know if I am.

Sophia stirs, asks if we're there yet. *We can be*, Jon says. *Just let us know where you wanna get out.* I kick the back of his seat. She reaches out to hand me something. My notebook. *You left this on the train.* I thank her, smell it for some reason, breathe in the sweet scent of worn paper. Her voice now. *Is she based on me.* I nod, then realise she's not looking at me. *You're a part of her*, I say. She's quiet a moment. *You might not realise it yet*, she says. *But it's her story.*

In our bubble, fear consumed me. I was scared I'd lose her. After she left, I was scared I'd made it happen. That I'd willed it somehow. Fear is as fear does. When you've only got one thing and you lose that thing, you lose everything. Life is consequences.

When it finally came, the end, it was a cul-de-sac disguised as a mews. I realised too late. There was no redirect, no recourse. After months of watching something implode in excruciating slow motion, I was very suddenly bereft, without consolation.

A thing I tell people is that Sophia was single when we met at the gig that night.

A thing I don't say is that there may have been some overlap with her ex.

Thirteen

Iowa / Anger, Part II

Lightning dances on the horizon. The storm must be hundred miles wide, a curtain of fire rippling staccato across the skyline. Bolts fire at random. Purples, blues, flashes of white flame, like the hypnotic charge of a plasma lamp. I reach back and tap Sophia on the leg, pointing at the horizon in answer to the inevitable, *What*. She rests her chin on the side of the car. We stay like that a while, watching the show in silence. The next time I look back I see she's fallen asleep again. Fisher is nestled into my legs, shaking. *It's okay, buddy*, I say, stroking the top of his head, keeping my eyes fixed on the faraway storm, thankful the thunder isn't closer.

The plains are made of a thousand fields, dust and dirt and grass and corn. Northern English moors, Australian outback, apple pie prairie, battered badland. Buildings are sporadic. The orange flame and black smog of a distant refinery. The occasional gas station. Petrol cathedrals. Only thing more abundant over here than churches. We pass one Paul and I found in Nebraska that had a counter papered with printed-out Internet jokes. There's one pulled from the road I grew up on, old mechanical pumps with flip clock displays that haven't spat fuel in years. Back beyond the occasional rest stop, the storm simmers on the edge of visible. Waiting. Coiled. Wind buffets the side of the car. The part of my mind we're passing through is anger.

Nothing much grows here.

That fighter pilot I read about, ejected at 50,000 feet into a storm cloud, spent forty minutes trapped inside, rising on updrafts, falling, rising again, covered in ice, bleeding from his eyes, his ears, until the storm let him go. You can fall for ever if the wind wants you to.

Jon checks she's sleeping. *So what, you're friends now.*
We're not not friends, I say. *But we're not enemies.*
I couldn't do it, not after all she's done to you.
What are you talking about, I say.
She tore you apart, he says.
And I did the same.

It's a clever plan, he says. *Have her break down, ride to the rescue.*
I tell him to shut up. He fiddles with the radio, half-listens to a few stations, switches it off again. *This way she needs you, right.* I start to tell him I didn't plan this. That I'm going to let her go. But I stop myself.

And what if I need her, I say.
He shrugs. *Then we've got a lot further to go.*

My superpower is selective vision. I can see what I want to from a hundred paces.

Jon is tense, terse. We're clashing, slipping like a worn clutch plate. Knocking heads. It's been a long couple of days. Tempers burning up on re-entry. Spend enough time with anyone you get sick of them. Spend enough time with yourself it just might kill you.

I'm twenty-two, ducking under a punch. Paul's fist connects above my right ear. A scuff. I don't know how the argument started, but I got out of the car. He wanted me to get back in.

Took a swing at me when I refused. We never much talked through our fights, never apologised for words or fists. Just waited till it was forgotten. A week later he was dead.

Time slips. Musical chairs. I'm in back. Sophia drives. The storm is on top of us. The wind makes the car swerve to keep a straight line. From the front seat I hear untruths and half quotes. The storm bathes them both in red light. Portraits in a dark room, lit only in flashes. Then a pitch in the frame rate. Their motion stuttered, animated. They skip and rewind and flicker. Fragments, figments. Everything is red. Lynch-like. I can't trust my eyes. I shut them tight and listen.

She says: *He knows what I'm going to do.*
She says: *And yet he lets me do it.*
He says: *He lies to himself.*
He says: *That's his superpower.*
She says: *What scares him more.*
She says: *That I won't leave, or that I will.*

Thunder now. What the thunder said was the thunder barked. The thunder laughed. Who's to say I can trust my ears. When I open my eyes it looks like they're holding hands.

I'm thirty-one, waiting to hear from her. It's late. I'm in bed. She's out somewhere. I stay awake, staring at my phone. I have to masturbate three times to fall asleep. When she calls, she's drunk in a cab. She apologises for not texting. *I love you,* she says. Her voice is soothing, sedative. Sometimes when you're too scared to sleep you just need to be read a story.

In our bubble she's trying to make a hollandaise. It's not going well. I'm a full-time grouch, but her bad moods creep up, all stealthy, unpredictable. This is usually how it starts, with her being frustrated she can't do something. On cue, she throws the saucepan in the sink, storms out in a tear-filled fury, insists she's never cooking again. I have different tactics for this. Today I try to make her laugh. When she comes back in, I'm holding a candlelight vigil for the hollandaise. I read a poem I wrote. Sometimes levity works. Those times she'll laugh, lighten up. This time, well. Let's just say I'm yet to find a better opponent in a game of let's not talk for four days.

Another tactic was to play Dashboard Confessional at full volume.

A thing I wonder: what came first, the Emo or the agony.

I sit up in my seat and Jon hands me his hip flask. *Drink deep,* he says. I sip cheap turps through clenched teeth. *You know when someone dies and the body evacuates its bowels,* I say. Jon nods. *Death shits.* I hand him back the flask. *That's the kind of shit I feel like.*

Tell me, she says. *What have you taken.*
Dunno, I say. *Don't remember it all.*
Jon speaks for me. *He's on ket.*
Ketamine, she says. *Really.*
Really. Whole heap of it.
But… but he doesn't—
He does. He did.

A meteorite flares above us. Burns bright, fades out, skips across the highway. The road ripples like water in its wake. I tell them about the hallucinogen. About the sleeping pills. *The whiskey,* Jon says. He knows what I know. *You took all that,* she says. She asks why, even though she knows what I know. *So I'd miss you.* I shake my head. *So I wouldn't miss you any more.*

Drugs never scared Sophia. She'd do white from time to time. At gigs. She'd arrive back from the bathroom, pupils like black holes, buzzing. She'd want to fool around. Not sure if it was the white or the thrill of doing it. But it upset me. I was too jealous, too insecure.

It's always guys that have white. Guys who carry just to be interesting. They'd offer. She'd go. I'd shake my head. *Not for me.* I was anxious, scared. Scared of being like them. Scared that white would make me more fun, more interesting. That she'd like me more if I did it.

I'm twenty-seven, being told I'm no fun. *You're no fun,* my wife says. *We never have fun.* Later I'll realise the depression was to blame. The way it flattened me. Made me too serious. But her words do damage. *You're no fun.* They hit me out of nowhere, a rock leaving ripples.

A thing I'm afraid of is being boring.

You could have called me, Sophia says. *If it was that bad.* I tell her it's not that simple. It's never that simple. *How hard is it to ask if I'm okay,* I say. *A year, and you never asked. Not once.* She looks hurt. *Don't confuse me not asking with me not giving a shit.* What I say next is, *Whatever,* because that's the worst thing you can say in an argument.

In 1978, a Russian surveillance satellite, Kosmos 954, crashed in northern Canada. Its nuclear core spread radioactive material over hundreds of miles. Only 0.1 per cent of the waste was ever recovered. It was meant to stay in orbit for a lifetime. It lasted four months.

Fisher whines, needs to stretch his legs. I'm about to tell them to pull over when Jon pipes up. *Fisher could use a run*, he says. We pull into a rest stop that looks like any in America. Parking bays, and picnic benches bolted into the floor. People will steal the fuck out of unsecured seating. I climb from the car. The air full of static and tension. *I'll get us a table*, Sophia says. She smiles at Jon as she goes and I realise she's glowing, but it's not for me.

What was that.
We're getting along.
You're getting along, I say.
Come on, he says. *Don't be that guy.*
Probably a little late for that at this point.
Is it a problem if I get along with your dog, too.

I'm thirty-one, feeling pretty low. I give her a choice. *If you do it, I do it.* She's excited now. Animated. *This will be so fun.* It is fun. She cuts lines and we stay in the cubicle, fuck each other's brains out. It feels so good. And it was so easy. That scares me more than anything.

I'm thirty-one, crashing. I make my excuses and leave. Sophia comes with me. As we go, a mutual friend of ours curses her out. *Why the fuck would you pressure him like that.* Sophia tells her she doesn't know what she's talking about. *He pressured me into giving him permission.*

The rest stop has a diner that's less of a building, more of a shack. A lean-to, held together by cooking grease and casual racism. I've been here once before, a pancake place nowhere near Iowa. A waitress brings over menus and bad news. *Dog's gonna have to stay outside.* Jon takes Fisher out to the car. Sophia opens her menu. I already know what she'll order.

In our bubble we're at brunch. Our weekend routine is we roll out of bed around twelve, eye sore, coffee shy, stumble to one of the north London cafes on our brunch rota. We stayed at mine, so she woke up in one of my shirts, my boxers. She's wearing them still, with her jeans, one of my jumpers. My clothes swamp her just enough to end wars. Until the coffee kicks in we sit and read our books. We always order the same thing: me, eggs royale; her, pancakes. And we always take a book. Sometimes novels. Mostly musician memoirs. Mostly bad. There are occasional highlights. Her favourite is Patti Smith, mine David Lee Roth. It's not that she loves biographies, it's that she figures she'll ghostwrite a few if the A&R thing doesn't work out. Someone nearby orders wine. *Too early to start drinking*, she says. I shake my head. *It's three thirty*. We order a bottle of prosecco, two bloody Marys. *Extra bloody*, she says, as the waiter walks off. *Extra Mary*, I say. She spits out her coffee. Mostly I spend my time trying to make her laugh.

Thinking about it, we drank a lot in our bubble.

Fireballs fall from the sky, dropping like pebbles in the parking lot. From the window I can see Fisher watching us from the back seat. I worry about him in this storm. Thunder makes the walls shake. A diner at the edge of the apocalypse. I think I'll have pancakes.

The waitress approaches with either caution or indifference. *What's the biggest coffee you serve*, Jon says. She points to the menu. *Bottomless horn*, she says. *You'll drown before you finish it.* Jon closes his menu, grinning. *Yeah, I'm gonna need one of those.*

There's always room for whimsy, is something she told me once.

I'm twelve, watching a detective drama with my parents. It's about a serial killer who lures women out of their cars at night by leaving childlike dolls in the road, then chases them through the woods. I didn't sleep properly for two weeks. I've never been so terrified.

Later that summer I hid under a sheet in my room because I was afraid of murderers. It was the middle of the day, the murderers weren't real. It didn't occur to me that I'd be really easy to spot under a sheet. It only occurred to me to hide.

That thing you read about covering a birdcage with a cloth to stop parrots getting scared at night. It cuts out visual stimulation.

In reality, out there, where she's flesh and want and not my imagination, she only did white a couple of times. Once with a musician hero of hers, once with me. I know because she told me. She never gave me any reason not to trust her. I found some anyway.

Jon's got the horn, and he's wrestling with it. *No one's ever drunk the whole thing*, the waitress says. *You finish it, your breakfast is free.* I'm pretty sure it's free anyway.

He says: *That's a lot of coffee.*
I say: *It's bottomless.*
He says: *Bullshit.*

Sometimes Mum would read us stories when we couldn't sleep. Myths. There was one where Loki tricks Thor into drinking from a horn he's attached to the ocean. Thor ends up drinking so much that he causes the seas to shift. In Norse mythology, that's where tides come from.

In our bubble she asks what depression feels like. *Like you're trying to drink the ocean*, I say.

People say breakfast is the most important meal of the day, but I don't agree. The most important meal of the day is the one you're eating. And there's nothing saying they can't all be breakfast.

I'm half a pancake through the stack when it begins. *We've been thinking*, Jon says. *Sophia and I.* He chooses his words carefully. I don't know this Jon, don't like him. I commit to my plate, push pancakes into my face. *And, well.* She picks up his slack. *You're going to help me leave*, she says. Jon tags back in. *It makes sense*, he says. *It's on the way.* I never order pancakes. I'm hunched over, white knuckled, shovelling. I find room for more. Maple syrup chin. Cake-clogged throat. So much for trying something new. *You're not well, chief.* She takes his words, runs with them. *You're a walking corpse.* I retch, mouth so full I can't chew. *Look at yourself*, she says. *I'm asking you, please. Let me go while you still can.* I finally manage to swallow.

You don't think I'll make it out.
It's not that, buddy, Jon says.
What is it then, I say.
That you don't want to.

When we broke up I sent her emails. She never replied. I sent her texts. Her answer was always the same: *I don't know what to say.*

I swipe the car keys and stride out of the diner into an electric squall, a curtain of lightning slung close, bolts of fire flashing several times a second, sans sequence. The static stands my hair on end. A red neon DINER sign explodes above me. I drop to my knees, adrenalin shakes, quivering, quickening. Synapses fire, heart flutters. I feel so alive.

What happens next is I projectile vomit blueberry pancakes all over the parking lot.

Spent, I lie supine, listening to the thunder, the occasional *clink* of rock on asphalt. Here, for the first time, beside a pool of my own vomit, in the middle of a storm in my mind, I lay myself open to the benign indifference of her words: *I don't know what to say.*

I'm twenty-two, on my road trip with Paul. We've seen 3,000 miles of highway and as many chain eateries before I realise that International House of Pancakes and IHOP are the same place.

The car now. They must have carried me. The fever kicks me around in a storm cloud. I shiver, cold sweat and calenture. Fisher licks my face. He likes the salt. In front they're laughing, flirting, flickering under street lamps. Fuckers. Fuck them both. I pass out.

Next time I come to, Jon's driving and Sophia sits in back with me, stroking my head. She used to do this when I was sick. *My turn to make you feel good*, she'd say. Here, I melt into her.

The scene won't stay still. Maybe because I don't believe it. Maybe she's in front with Jon.

Her voice. *Did he ever tell you about Paul.*
Sure, Jon says. *Died behind the wheel.*
Then he told it wrong, Sophia says.
What are you saying, Jon says.

My voice. I mumble. Words aren't working. *You're in bad shape there, partner,* Jon says. I tell him to shut up. He's not hearing me. Not trying to. *Listen,* he says. I interrupt. *Shut the fuck up, Pete.* Jon finds me in the rear view. *Sorry, champ,* he says, *your brother ain't here.*

A thing I never say is that my brother and I haven't spoken in a decade.

A thing I never say is that I was driving the night Paul died.

Fourteen

The Gate

Add an obstacle here. It's dawn when I notice the car has stopped. It should be dawn, at least. This is day three. There's no sun. Not one we can see. The clouds are too thick. Sounds now. The whirr and screech of windscreen wipers across glass. The percussive hum of raindrops on the roof. I always listen to rain when I write, drowns out distractions. In front, something is blocking the beam from our headlamps. I lean forward in my seat. A wall. I can't see the top. There's a portcullis, wrought iron, archaic. Where's Fezzik when you need him.

The thing with night is that the sun's still shining, it just isn't shining on you.

Whirr. Sophia sits in the driving seat, both hands on the wheel. *Did you put this here,* she says. Screech. I squint and blink and rub my eyes, tell her I didn't. She groans, frustrated, tugs at the wheel. Jon puts a hand on her shoulder. My organs sink. He speaks. *You know that all this is you, right.* I tell him it isn't me. *Then who the fuck is it,* Sophia says. Whirr. I nod ahead, into the path of the headlights. Screech. The Many-Faced Man leans against the gate, arms folded, heel resting on the grille. He grins at us. Face and form shifting. The pose, the posture; he looks a lot like Jon. *There you go, Doc,* I say. *There's your Ringo.* Whirr. Another figure steps into the light, stands next to the Many-Faced Man. A man with none. Screech.

She says: *What the fuck is that.*
I say: *A wrong I can't right.*
Jon says: *Real nice, kid.*
She says: *Is that—*
I say: *Paul.*

Whirr. Screech.

Sophia turns the wipers off. The windscreen becomes an abstract landscape, images it held blurred beyond recognition. Ink on blotting paper. A lesser Rothko. *So his face just—* She touches her nose to check it's still there. *Disintegrated,* I say. Her fingers trace her lips. I try not to watch. She exhales. *You made a monster of him.* I miss her mouth. My heart is rolling through my chest like a skydiver in a storm cloud. I nod. *And a beast of myself.*

Fisher chews my hand. He knows not to bite. *We should see what they want,* Sophia says. Jon volunteers. *I've got this.* It sounded like he said the word *babe.* She looks at me. *You're just going to let him go.* Jon pushes his door open. *He goes out there, this whole thing gets ugly.* I ask if he's sure. *Hey,* he says, climbing out of the car, *I'm your Huckleberry.*

Fisher yawns. I let him drink water from a bottle I didn't know I had. Ahead, Jon is talking with the Many-Faced Man. It looks like Paul is trying to mediate. Hooded wrongs gather round the gate, watching. Guarding. Her voice. *Did you think that maybe when I texted you to ask about something else, what I was really doing was checking you were okay.*

Was it all a lie, I say. *The bubble, everything in it.*
Why would you say that. Of course it was real.

Then why did you change your mind, I say.
Minds change. You said you'd let me go.
I will, I say. *I wasn't quite ready then.*
Jon said you were just saying that.
I wanted to believe I meant it.
Then you know how it feels.

The door swings open and a soaking wet Jon plants himself down in the passenger seat. Fisher stands up, excited. He thinks this is a game. Maybe it is. Jon flips open his flask and takes a swig. *Yeah they aren't gonna open the gate.* I ask if they want something. He nods. *Bingo.* Sophia is impatient. *Well, what is it.* Jon hikes a thumb at Fisher. *They want the D-O-G.* I put my hands over his ears. *Hey,* I say. *He can spell.* Fisher is panting happily, I'm pretty sure he can't spell. There is always room for whimsy. *What do they want with him,* Sophia says. Jon looks at her. *Same thing you do, I think,* he says. I ask what he means.

Jon's voice. *Show him.* She pulls a folded piece of paper from her pocket and gives it to me. It's a photocopy of a photocopy of a picture of Fisher. It has the headline MISSING DOG in thick black font. Ariel, I think. People are always making poor font choices. Under the picture it says *big reward* in slightly smaller font. The kerning is off. There's no other info. No phone number. I ask her what it is, apart from the obvious. *A ticket out of here,* she says. *If I deliver the dog, I can leave.* I ask if she believes that. *No reason not to,* she says. She takes it back, folds it away.

Maybe Jon was right. That I keep making it so she needs me. She has the key. She has a car. She doesn't need me. I'm just slowing her down. I'm being selfish. *We could always jump the wall,* Jon says. *Some kind of trebuchet.* His eyes light up. *I always wanted to build a siege engine.*

Fisher puts his paw in my lap. I take it in my hand, kiss his head. Breathe him in. *Good boy.*

White noise washes over the car. Grey shapes move unseen. I open my notebook at random, read from the top. *What if there is a finite amount of happiness to go around and every bit of happiness you take for yourself is happiness you take from someone else.*

Every book is a self-help book if you read it right.

I'm out of the door before anyone can stop me. Weak-kneed, wrong-footed. Unsteady but upright. I lean into the wind and hang on to a hat I'm not wearing. Three or four paces and my T-shirt is already drenched. Lightning like a bad horror movie. Jon races after me. *What are you doing, partner.* Wrongs crowd round the road. It narrows as their numbers grow. Some shout as I stumble past. Someone starts a chant. *Nobody likes you. Everybody hates you. Eat a bag of dicks.*

Jon holds my shoulders, looks me in the eyes, understands. *I gotta see a man about a dog,* I say. What he understands is that I'm doing this. That he can't change my mind. *Well, you know what they say,* he says. He does the pause thing, rain battering us both. *He who makes a man of himself gets rid of the pain of being a beast.* He claps my shoulder and makes his way back to the car. *Hey,* I say. *Look after my dog.* The coolest man I've ever known, even in a category four storm.

You look like shit, the Many-Faced Man says, his face a fruit machine that won't settle, his voice an oddly modulated mix of several. He continues. *You know when someone dies and they shit themselves.* I interrupt. *Come on,* I say. *You can do better. Tell me I look like part-baked ciabatta.* He laughs. *Say I look like the pile of shit getting fisted in* Jurassic Park. They're all laughing now. All my wrongs. I spin an imaginary gun, holster it. *I have not yet begun to defile myself.*

He walks towards me. Saunters. Taunts. His features sit unimpressed in multiple. *Have you put on weight,* he says. His frame is large, but trimmer than mine. Fitter. The crowd close ranks. *How about you open the gate,* I say. I see familiar faces. A boss from an old job. A girl I ghosted. Some shout. *Fraud. Fool. Fuck-up.* Others sneer. *What was with the cowboy,* he says. I shrug, tell him Jon's my tour guide. *He said he was your attorney.* He circles me, sizes me up. *I'll make you a deal,* I say. *Let us through, and nobody has to get hurt.* What happens next is the kind of laughter that makes you wince. It's every laugh I've ever hated. It's all directed at me.

He says: *Did he tell you what happens if you die in here.*
He says: *You know they're fucking, right.*
He says: *You're a dead man.*

In the distance, a neon sign burns against the horizon: *Mostly dead is slightly alive.*

How building tension works is you have to flip the power. Reverse it. I stumble, steady myself, set my feet. I breathe deep, let the laughter seep through until I'm shaking with Tetsuo rage. High above a space rock spins through the air, falling towards us, towards him. He stops laughing and looks up, sees me. His faces wash with fear. The rock flies over my head and hits him square in the chest. It drops to the ground with a *clink*. It's the size of a pebble. He is unmoved. I exhale, drop to my knees, exhausted. He looks at the pebble, laughs louder than before, harder.

He strides towards me, grabs the back of my head. His faces inches from mine, rage shining from each. *Here's a deal,* he says. *Give me the dog, and I'll make us great again.* He holds me by the throat, his faces shifting back and forth like a hologram card pulled from a cereal box.

Then it clicks. Who these faces belong to. Who I'm fighting. *It's my turn,* he says. His many faces, all of them mine, spin from laughter to anger to smug triumph. *You had your chance,* he says. He is me. He knows that I know, sees it on my face. The look of horror I can't hide.

He smiles. *You've fucked it,* he says. *You're done. Time I showed the world who we really are.* He drops me, steps back. *Lucky for you I need you alive,* he says. *Lucky for me, not too alive.*

He waves his hand and my wrongs crowd around, bear down with fists, feet. I try to cover up. *Enough,* I say. More to hear the word, to practise it. Louder now. *Enough.* With the last of my strength I stand, push back. Fists raised. Lightning strikes everywhere at once, a flash that makes the crowd cover their eyes, cower. *Enough,* I say, because that's all I've practised.

What Jon also understood when he looked in my eyes was that I wanted him to go, to forget about me, to help her. What I was saying was simple: *I can't do this with you here.*

I close my eyes. Her voice. *It never would have lasted.* A fireball blazes overhead. A mortar. A missile. A meteor. Memories scatter. It's big. The Many-Faced Man moves as the rock hits the ground where he stood, exploding on impact. A ball of flame, fury. The blast rips a hole in the wall, destroys the gate, throws wrongs to the floor. I spit out dirt, blood.

Enough.

Sophia guns it. Tyres screech on asphalt. I watch them through the smoke as they pass. She doesn't look for me. Jon waves. I nod. *Go.* They peel through the gate, the road beyond unfolding for her, stretching out into a distant dark. Fisher fogs the rear window, his face fading from view as the car grows smaller. *Bye, buddy*, I say, so quiet I barely hear it.

I hobble towards the hole in the daytime dark. Up close I see the wall is paper thin, perforated. Cardboard. Like a film set. Not easily scaled or detoured, but sodden, wrinkled. Wet enough to punch through. There's an analogy here. Soaking, sick, I stumble through the gate.

A man crosses a map of his memory.

I can't do this with you here.

He is alone.

Fifteen

Illinois / Jealousy

I'm an hour into a ten-day walk when the lights go out. It's a walk I'll be nine days dead by the time I finish. A walk I'll suffer in darkness. Colourful spots dance in front of my eyes, leading the way. After twenty minutes I realise I'm just walking with my eyes closed.

The weather situation is this: the rain has stopped. It's still day three. I think. It should be mid-morning but it's hard to tell in the dark. I can't see any clouds. There's nothing blocking the sun. It just isn't there. The thing with night is the sun's still shining, it just isn't shining on you.

My feet slap the road. Underfoot the sound turns hollow. A bridge. I don't know what it spans. The hole is either too deep to see, or the water too black. I find a stick and drop it over one side, shuffling to the other to watch it float past. It never does. No splash, no river, no stick.

There is a whale in the ocean that sings at a different frequency to other whales. He swims, follows the currents, sings, but he never gets an answer. The others can't hear him. Researchers first heard him in the eighties. They've no idea how old he is, how long he's been out there, alone.

The bridge is made of wood. Old oak, framed by zig-zagging

struts on either side, a metal guard rail running at waist height, the deck wide enough for two lanes of traffic. There aren't any cars right now. It creaks. Talking to me. Maybe trying to talk to other bridges. Maybe it creaks at the wrong frequency. Maybe the other bridges can't hear it.

I'm ten, being dumped for the first time. I spend the entire lunch break walking around the playground, asking her, *Why*. Over and over. *Why*. I get the same answer every time. *Why*. She says she doesn't know. *Why*. She tells me to leave her alone. *Why*. I don't understand.

I'm twelve and my second girlfriend is dumping me. It's a week after Valentine's Day. She gives me back the card I got her, in its envelope. She screwed it up, spat in it. I run home in tears.

That thing your therapist said about repeating the same set of mistakes over and over.

The wind carries whispers, wails. *I can't do this with you here.* Jon and Sophia must be sixty miles away. Maybe a hundred, knowing Jon. They're out there together. Laughing, flirting. I can't do this with them. But, feet failing me, I'm not sure I can do it without them either.

Just because I'm imagining all of this doesn't make it any less real.

After she left I spent weeks lying foetal, sobbing. Haunted by the echo of questions I couldn't quiet. It was the why of it all I couldn't deal with; *Why. Why now. Why not me.* I didn't have answers, so I fashioned some. Despairing, desperate, the answers I formed were worse than any she could give. I fixed on a truth that began to demolish the past, to destroy all that was good.

The truth I conjured was this: *If she cheated with me, she must have cheated on me.*

My Chuck Taylors squeak, squelch. Waterlogged socks, cold feet. Chucks almost always have holes. You've barely bought a pair before they wear through and your feet are soaking wet. Both of the T-shirts I'm wearing are still damp. I'm getting a rash walking in wet jeans. I lean out over the rail and am hit flush in the face by a draught of hot air. I stick my hand out, let the hot air support its weight, my arm snaking along the upstream current.

Never let vanity get in the way of a good idea. I remove both my shirts and hang them over the edge, letting the rising heat dry them. I walk along, shirtless, arm outstretched, fabric flapping in the breeze. I look at my body. It's less impressive when not decorated with her lips, but hardly unsightly. It's lived in, is all. A body with stories. A narrative told in scar tissue. In tattoos and topography. Once my shirts dry, I pull them back on, strip to my boxers, hang my jeans and socks and shoes over the edge. A head full of hot air is a terrible thing to waste.

It's a funny thing, black. By definition both a colour and an absence of colour.

Maybe depression is the same. Not a feeling at all, but an absence of any.

I'm eleven, on a family holiday. I meet a girl who's my girlfriend for a week. When I leave we never officially break up. I spend the whole year unsure whether I had a girlfriend or not. The following summer she says we weren't going out in the first place. This is a relief. I wasn't ready for a girlfriend. The reason I thought she was my girlfriend is I fixed her bike.

I'm twenty-two, on the road with Paul. In Arizona, I use Myspace to message a girl I met when I was fifteen, on holiday in France. She replies a few days later, half-bemused, half-worried. *Is everything okay.* I didn't consider how weird it might be to hear from a guy you fooled around with for a week when you were fourteen. Paul laughs. *Probably time to let that one go.*

One man's romance is another man's restraining order.

Re-clothed, I continue. The bridge is without end. The wind asks, *Why.* It repeats as I walk, legs leaden, lactic. *Why, why, why.* The exhaust blowing from below moans, a sexually satisfied purr. Her voice. *You make me feel so good.* A metal cord whips against the pole. A black flag hangs at half-staff, as if the bridge is in mourning. It's dark and hell is twenty-two degrees.

My notebook sits rolled in my hand, frayed, stained. I use it to conduct the wind, play a drum beat against the handrail. I'm supposed to be working on a novel. Things keep getting in the way. Walls. Bridges. When I started writing it, I wanted it to be so good she'd come back. I wanted to make her fall in love with me. Words don't work like that, especially when you don't write them.

The worst thing I've ever written was the email I sent when she broke things off. It was a considerable fuck of a mess. I misquoted her, misinterpreted things, bent facts. Changed contexts. I quoted John F. Kennedy and the film *Say Anything* in the same paragraph.

What I got in return was a text message: *I'm sorry. I don't know what else to say.*

In November 2014, after ten years in space, the Philae lander launched from the spacecraft *Rosetta* and successfully landed on a comet. The first human-made craft ever to do so. He set about his tasks, taking soil samples, analysing them like a champ. But his battery began to dwindle rapidly and on 15 November he stopped communicating. Scientists feared the worst. Then in June 2015, *Rosetta* received a transmission. Philae had woken up. He resumed his final task: transmitting chemical data. *Rosetta* lost contact with him shortly after. Without enough solar energy to stay awake, he powered down and died, cold and alone, marooned in space.

My email should have been six words long; *I love you, I always will.*

Animism is the belief that inanimate objects have feelings.

My superpower is putting my foot in it.

I'm thirty-one and Sophia is telling me about a guy at work. *He's beautiful.* Later she texts me instead of him. *Oops, not for you.* I get angry, kick up a fuss. Not my finest hour. She says she's not into him. I can only hear, *He's beautiful.* She says I'm being an idiot. Maybe I am.

The thought I can't get out of my head is, *What if I'm not.*

There's always overlap.

I trip, tired. Tardy. Running late for my own oblivion. Where's a sensible family minivan when you need one. I take stock. I must only be midway across. I can't catch them. Can't have her back. Maybe a fall will wake me up. Maybe a fall will kill me. I never did ask what happens if I die up here. I breathe in. Motor oil, defeat. Weigh my options. There's only wind and the void.

The choice makes itself: it's easier to fall than to walk. I climb up on to the rail, turn inward, face the deck. I think about her lips, about the last time I kissed her. I didn't know it'd be the last. Maybe she knew. Maybe she'd planned it, savoured it. I lean out slightly. Her voice rises on the air: *It never would have lasted.* I spread my arms like wings, close my eyes, fall backward.

It's not suicide if you're trying to fly.

People talk about rock bottom. Say you reach it eventually, then you can climb back up. I don't believe in rock bottom. You can fall as long as you want. You can just keep falling.

Here, now, I land flat on my back. The abyss is a hard surface sitting inches below the bridge.

My notebook lies nearby, sitting next to the stick I dropped, both suspended on the same solid nothing, a barrier so black it appears infinite. I flip through my notes, find a line: *Talk about silence. Say the happiest you've ever been was reading quietly with her.*

The happiest times were the ones when we both read quietly, lying across each other like dropped matches, the sound of paper friction, pages turning, satisfied bodies shifting weight, being, breathing. Here, in the black of my mind, suspended, I feel her lie back on my chest, fingers combing flaxen hair, happy groans, stolen glances, stolen kisses. I remember every detail.

The only trouble is I'm not sure if it happened. Not like this. Memory is mostly invention. I don't remember what I remember. Maybe the silences weren't happy. Maybe I made this up. I mean, I never met her parents. We never had a holiday, never invited friends round for dinner parties. We fucked and drank and made promises and maybe we were never part of the same story.

That thing you read, that your friends might not consider you their friends.

Other things I may have invented: our past, our present, our future.

Fiction is the only time the loser gets to write history.

Dazed, I climb back up to the bridge, lie foetal on the road. The deck creaks, rolls. I scroll through things she told me: *You make me feel so good. He's beautiful. It never would have lasted.*

I think she actually said, *It was always going to end*, but I prefer, *It never would have lasted.*

I take the pen from my pocket, hold it like a child might, nib protruding from the back of my fist. I find a fresh page and start carving, scratching words into the pulp. *You make me feel so good. I don't know what to say. I'm sorry.* My handwriting is rough, illegible. It doesn't matter. I just want the words to exist. I keep going: *He's so beautiful. I love you, I'm gonna come.* I tear out the page, push it between a crack in the deck, pull a Zippo I didn't know I had from my pocket, flick it open, light it. The paper smokes, smoulders. Fleeting yellow flame. Then nothing. Cotton tendrils rise in wisps from the black edges of the page. I roll on to my back, defeated.

Words don't burn so easy.

What annoyed me about her: she talked too loudly on buses, so other people had to listen. She had different personalities for different friends. She had a fake phone voice. She asked questions in the cinema. Every now and then she chewed with her mouth open. She's a really good liar.

What really annoyed me about her: I hated how attracted I was to her.

Other words for bubble: blip, bead, blister.

There's an elephant at a Tokyo zoo that has spent sixty-six years living in a concrete pen. She's known as the loneliest elephant in the world. Campaigners started a petition to get her released, but experts said she wouldn't have survived a move. Captivity is all she knows.

That thing you read about lonely people dying sooner.

Through squinting eyes, shooting stars fly sideways along the road, roll past, screech to a stop. Turns out stars smell like gasoline. A door opens. Not stars, just passing headlights. Then a voice. Jon. *What's this*, he says. *The dark night of the goddamn soul.*

He lifts my arm, wraps it round his neck, picks me up. The car sits close by, just out of focus. It's a minivan, the one Paul and I once took on a US road trip. Gary Busey. What are the chances. He props me in the passenger seat, pulls my legs into the car one by one, the way you would for someone without much use of his limbs. I let him buckle my seat belt. *Gets bumpy*, he says.

My favourite death on the BASE Fatality List is an honourable mention. Dwain Weston was a world champion BASE jumper, but for the Go Fast Games in Colorado, 2003. Weston and his buddy Jeb Corliss planned to do a fly-by of the Royal Gorge Bridge wearing wing suits. Weston would fly over the top of the bridge. Corliss underneath. As they approached the bridge Weston was flying low, but spectators assumed he'd pull up at the last second. He didn't. He hit a railing at 120mph, severing his leg and killing him on impact. Jeb, who flew underneath as planned, was showered with Weston's blood, almost colliding with the body as it fell from the bridge.

Some BASE jumpers said Weston wasn't used to piloting the wingsuit and lost control. Others thought maybe he'd tried to aim for a two-metre gap between railings, to raise the stakes.

They say it's the fall that kills you. For Dwain Weston it was the bridge itself.

It's not suicide if it's an accident. It's death by misadventure.

But you left, I say. *You drove off with Sophia.*
You didn't give me a choice, Jon says.

A face that isn't appears behind me. Paul. *She's not worth the trouble, mate*, he says, sinew and muscle straining to show emotions they can't translate without skin. He lithpth a little, but that's to be expected for a man without lips. *But you were with him*, I say. *That other me.* He waves it off. *I'd rather be here*, he says. *You're a bit of a cunt, but less of a cunt than he is.*

I think he winks at me, but without eyelids it's hard to say for certain.

Jon starts the engine. The timbre under the wheels changes as we leave the deck and hit solid road. *Thought I'd never get off that bridge,* I say. *Was walking for hours.* He and Paul laugh, hard and hearty. *You're kidding, right,* Jon says. *Damn thing's fifty feet across.*

The next sound I hear is my own delirious laughter.

The wind: *I can't do this with you here.*

On the dash, an E.T. bobblehead doll nods at us, keeping time with the sway of the chassis. He was our mascot, back then. We picked him up at a Walmart in Pennsylvania. It made sense, the three of us being alien tourists in a foreign land. He was also a good reminder to phone home.

Jon is quiet. He's not even drumming. I ask if he's mad at me. A minute slips by, words hang unanswered. *You push,* he says. *All the time. And you wonder why people leave. It gets tiring, champ.* He leans close, whispers. *And just between us, having me go on without you made zero sense, narratively speaking. Terrible choice.* He smiles now. *Butch ain't shit without Sundance.*

In another life, Jon would have made a hell of an editor.

That thing you read about the blackest material ever created, a kind of carbon that absorbs 99.9 per cent of light. It's so black the human eye can't comprehend it. You can be looking at a surface less than a millimetre thick and think you're staring into a bottomless abyss.

In back, Paul is digging through a box of cassette tapes. *Can I ask you something,* I say. *What do you live for when you've got nothing left*. He's quiet a moment, pensive. Tyres thud over asphalt cracks. *Dunno*, he says. *Think maybe you're asking the wrong person.*

When you're busy remembering the worst about somebody, it's easy to forget why you were friends in the first place. I ask him why he's here, after what I did. Globs of viscera drip syrup-like from his open wound of a face. *You find monsters where you look for them.*

If he had skin he'd probably be grinning.

Sixteen

Indiana / Jealousy

Jon drives. Paul plays deejay. I'm in back. It's day four. When I'm not sleeping, billboards littered along the blacktop sell me a life I'll never have. Some of the posters show me, a future me, smiling; Sophia drunk. We pose in carefully curated holiday photos. In some we have kids. She does, at least. I watch as my picture fades in each. Overlapped by other men, other lives.

If we were on our road trip we'd be somewhere in Illinois. A road sign points to Chicago. On our trip we barely drove through, we were tired, fed up of sightseeing. *Said we'd see it next time,* Paul says. *Lots we never got to do.* He fumbles with a cassette, pushes it into a slot that shouldn't be in the dash. Arcade Fire. A nice surprise. Paul never had the best taste in music. He lost his virginity in the back of his dad's Transit van to 'Senza Una Donna' by Paul Young.

Some people find my taste in music depressing. My ex-wife did. Sophia listened to the first mixtape I made her over and over. *It's beautiful and sad,* she said. *Like all the best things.*

That thing you read about sad music actually making people happier. Something to do with letting you process your sadness, instead of ignoring it. Happy music is a form of denial.

The mixtape for this would be: *How to kill friends and effluence people.*

I sleep well in cars. The vibrations always send me off soundly. Here, now, I pass in and out. Exhausted, fatigued, car tired. In front, Paul and Jon banter like old friends. Maybe they are. I close my eyes to the sound of a song about waking up.

The next time I open my eyes, I move to stretch out, roll my neck, only to jump at a body next to mine. Sophia. She's on her phone, texting. She's glowing, but not for me. From the front, Paul and Jon are talking, don't notice I'm awake. Don't notice that Sophia is here. Maybe she isn't. She laughs and plays with her hair and I hate how much I wish she were here.

A road sign points to the twin cities of Agony and Bliss.

In the weeks before the bubble burst, Sophia starts acting strangely with her phone. She puts it down when I walk in the room. Replies to texts when she thinks I'm sleeping. There are nights when I don't hear from her at all. She works late. Record label shit. But what happens is I start to think maybe it isn't work. The more I think about it, the more convinced I become.

When she breaks up with me I know it's because she's found someone else. A co-worker. An ex. Something easy. Something sans feelings, sans strings. I need it to be true. There's always overlap. If she's fucking someone else I can be upset, angry. I get to be the victim.

The alternative, that she just fell out of love with me, is too upsetting to contemplate.

A hand on my forehead. *Here, love, drink this.* My mum. She tilts a bottle to my lips. I shut my eyes. Mum asks what's wrong. I can't keep track, memories slip, shift. *I'm tired, Mum,* I say. She checks my forehead. *You don't have a temperature, love. Maybe you should get some sleep.*

I'm thirty-one, at my parents' house. Sophia broke up with me three days ago. I got on a train. Needed my mum. She brings me water, checks my temperature. *Your dad could use a hand in the garden if you're up to it,* she says. I roll over, stare at my phone. My stomach feels foreign, like a transplant my body is rejecting. *Why doesn't she want me,* I say. Mum pats my hand. *I'm sure your dad can manage without you.*

The break-up was our third. The first two times we didn't get far. A day or two before we caved, gave in. The first two were in person. We cried, went our separate ways, only to collide again when willpower wore thin. The third was via text. You can't see tears over text, can't see hearts shatter. Can't see how your words, simply stated, can crush completely.

The perma-dusk plays host to a mix of suburban sprawls, all borrowed from places I've lived: the high rises of London, the tenements of Manhattan, the terraced houses of my Yorkshire youth, the suburbs of Los Angeles. Buildings contract and swell as we pass, as if they're breathing. Whole city blocks rise and fall like the metal pins in one of those executive toys.

I'm cold. I find a bag in back, rummage through it, grab a black T-shirt. I pull it on over the other two. It's a Tomorrow Knights shirt. They had a couple of catchphrases. *For a better tomorrow* was one. This T-shirt features the other in a neon graffiti font: *It's Knight time.*

Paul asks about my brother. *He's good,* I say. Jon shakes his head. *They don't talk,* he says. *Not since you died.* He doesn't take his eyes off the road. I look at Paul. *It's not that*, I say. *We've just been busy.* Paul rubs what's left of his lower mandible. *Chinny reckon.* That's what a ten-year-old says when they know you're lying. In the passenger seat, Jon strokes his chin along with Paul.

My brother was Paul's friend too. As kids we rode bikes, climbed trees. Chased girls. As teenagers, Paul was the glue that kept us together. Until the crash. I moved to London after that. Pete didn't have anything to say to me. A month turned into a year, a year into two. He didn't come to my wedding. He teaches high school English. He's married, has a kid. He wrote a book.

I'm not sure if he wrote a book because he wanted to be a writer, or if he did it just to spite me.

I slip in and out to stereo sounds, to Jon singing. Suburbs give way to farmlands. Above, satellites twinkle like stars, each a dream, a hope, slowly drifting across the night sky. I think about Sophia, wonder where she is. Out there, in here. I think about how many of those satellites were launched by her. How many moon shots I took that never left orbit.

A song ends and I brace myself for the next. I know what it's going to be. I made this tape. One of Jon's. A favourite. The opening chords give me goosebumps still, more than twenty years after I first heard it. He moves to turn it off, but I tell him to leave it. We listen a moment.

I let the lyrics sink in, tears gathering. *Shit*, I say. *You made it sound so simple, you know. I grew up believing this stuff. That if you loved someone enough everything would be okay.* Jon turns down the volume. *Sometimes it's that simple*, he says. *And sometimes a song's just a song.*

As it rises into the second chorus, I watch the volume dial spin, hear it climb louder, feel it vibrate through the speakers in the door. Jon twists it, tries to turn it off, but nothing happens. Around us, satellites fall like snowflakes, sparkling against the night sky, scattering across fields and farms, setting the landscape on fire. Jon swerves to avoid a solar panel in the road. He pulls over, and we watch the light show. The night glows orange around us. It's raining dreams.

Paul turns in his seat, his lack of face showing something like concern. His shirt is spattered with blood. Pink spittle sprays from his mouth as he speaks. *All this is over a girl,* he says. I tell him he wouldn't understand. *What you asked earlier,* he says. *Is it not enough just to live.*

I'm thirty-one and Sophia is breaking my heart for the first time. I can barely stand. The words I manage are forced through tears. *I don't have anything without you.* She sobs and collapses into a chair. *I'm sorry. I'm so sorry.* I can taste salt as she tells me she didn't mean for it to end like this.

I ask her not to do this. She already has. We hug goodbye. The feel of her body pressed against mine gets me hard. She feels me stir and pulls back. *Sorry,* I say. *Instinct.* Hard-ons are mostly inappropriate. I grab my coat. It's raining out. I make it a block before I break down in tears.

Three days later dinner turns into drunken kissing in the street. We stumble home into bed, stripping, laughing, happy to feel something other than the crippling grief of goodbye.

Paul ejects the tape and the satellite storm ends. Light from the flames flickers across our faces, or our lack thereof. It's like watching the sun rise, a thousand small fires simulating a star creeping over the edge of the horizon. Turns out hope burns bright.

What I don't tell them is that Sophia is sitting next to me in back, glowing. Between us, a girl, no more than two years old. Our girl. I blink away a tear, and she's gone.

Paul says: *Try to win her back.*
I say: *There's nothing to win.*

I'm thirty-one, she's breaking up with me for the second time. It's a hot summer night and we're drunk. I see her phone light up, I get angry. She baulks. *I can't do this any more.* I apologise. We cry, console each other, roll to opposite sides of the bed. I fall asleep quickly, exhausted from tears.

In the morning I feel her lips press into mine. She rolls into me, plays little spoon, pushing her arse back, probing. I get hard quickly, pull her face around, kiss her. We smell of sleep and sweat and stale breath. I slide a hand into her knickers, let my fingers hover between her lips. She nods. *Yes.* I slide my fingers into her cunt, curling them slowly as she sighs and rolls back into me. I pull at her knickers, at my boxers, we push them down, kick them off. She straddles me, flesh on bare flesh. My hands gauge her hip bones, guiding her on to me. I claw at her, digging, gripping, rocking her body into mine. Grunting, wet slaps. She kisses me, bites my neck. I cry in pain, grab a fistful of her hair, pull her head back. I hold her there. Desperate, necessary. *Fuck. Yes. Fuck.*

She grinds against me, my cock solid inside her, swelling still. I pull her hair, press my hand to her throat. Her face burns red, sweat dripping between us. Friction, clenched teeth: *Fuck*. I loosen my grip, let her draw breath. She holds it, rocks harder against me, pushing me closer to the edge. My fingers dig into her hips. Her whole body is tense, shaking. Then: *I'm gonna come*. Her eyes roll back as she bucks, lets fly with a loud, *Fuck*. I've been clenching my teeth, holding back, but her orgasm tips me over. She can feel it. *Come for me, baby*, she says. I speed up, groan, go rigid, unload inside her. She sighs, slows her hips. Then we're still, sticky hot, panting. We lie intertwined. I stroke her hair, kiss her softly, watch beads of sweat run between her breasts. Later, over brunch, in the sober glow of morning, we decide to keep things going.

If you really want to fuck someone up, love them as hard as you can. I loved her so hard she couldn't breathe. My email should have been five words: *I suffocated you. I'm sorry*.

I persuade them to let me take a turn at the wheel. Jon reclines in back. Paul rides shotgun. It's hard to tell if he's resting or not. He doesn't have eyelids. Or eyes, really. Just dark holes where they used to be. Blood drips from the sockets like tears. His is a face in mourning for itself.

The car is in cruise. I'm only steering. That's mostly how people drive, steering themselves down highways, through lives. Paul stirs, asks if I'm okay. *I know I said I wanted to go back*, I say, *but what's waiting for me out there*. Paul shakes his head. *Have a day off or something. It's tiring*.

I bite the nail off my index finger in a perfect arc. In my rear view, I see imaginary passengers in the back seat, changing with the blink of tired eyes. My mum now. *How many great loves do you think you have*, I say. She looks like she might cry. *As many as your heart can take*.

The highway is built from huge preformed slabs dropped into place like toy bricks. The tyres make a *dum dum* noise as we roll over the seams between each. *I think people are like alloys,* my dad says. *You make each other stronger.* He tells me I'm speeding. *What's the opposite of an alloy,* I say. When I look up, Sophia sits where my dad was. She's looking at me sideways: *Do you ever think you're depressed because secretly, deep down, you want to be.*

Dum dum.

My brother's book was called *Excursion*. We pass a billboard advertising it. There's a quote from Stephen King: *Better than his fucking brother can do, that's for sure.*

The book is about Paul. Technically it's about a group of teen misfits, left behind while their classmates are on a field trip, who have to fight off an alien who crashes on school grounds. But it's based on him and Paul. Mum sent me a copy. I asked her what it was about. *Friendship,* she said. It sold well enough, was reviewed by a couple of papers. The *Guardian* said it was competent. The posters said it was *The Breakfast Club* meets *Aliens.* Everything is derivative.

Dum dum.

Jon is out cold in the seat behind me. Paul snores, which is understandable. We drive in silence until Sophia suggests a sing-along. She's not really here, but I indulge her. *What do you know,* I say. It takes us ten minutes to find the only song we both know the lyrics to: 'Mr Brightside'. *Well,* I say. *It did start with a kiss.* She laughs. It hurts in the good way.

The mixtape for this would be: *Songs to Keep You the Fuck Awake.*

Mum used to sing to us at bedtime. The first songs I loved weren't popular music, they were hers. The ones her mother used to sing to her. She'd tuck us in, serenade us to sleep. The one I liked best was about Christopher Robin. I always thought I'd sing it to my kids someday.

When she'd finish singing she'd ask if we were asleep. Sometimes we'd say yes and laugh. Sometimes we'd pretend to sleep, squinting through barely open eyes. She could always tell, but she didn't mind. She used to say the best way to fall asleep is to close your eyes and pretend.

I asked her to stop singing to me, eventually. I was eight, suddenly embarrassed. Desperate to cast off childish things. I bet it broke her heart. Kids will just about ruin you. Ask your parents.

Someone slaps my arm from the back seat. *What the fuck.* I jerk awake. *Were you sleeping.* My brother, Pete. I shake my head. *Of course not.* His form fades away. I roll down the window, sit up in my seat, flagging, failing, in no state to drive.

Somewhere in my mind, Mum is singing me to sleep. A song she used to sing when we were very young. Back when the best way to fall asleep was by pretending. I let my eyelids fall shut. All is peaceful as the car sails across lanes, the soft ripples of memory in our wake.

Dum dum.

Seventeen

Pennsylvania / Violence

The clock on the dash blinks eights. Each a thud, an echo. I wonder if it's trying to communicate, if it's a code I can't read. Above, the night sky is absent all light. No moon. No stars. The scene is lit entirely by hazard bulbs, strobing orange, a warning for something that's already happened.

An air bag lies half inflated in front of me. Rousing, I realise I'm covered in blood, broken glass. The windshield is shattered. My face feels numb, my nose tender. I don't think it's broken. I try to pull my seat belt off, it gives on the third go. I find my collar bone sore, my neck stiff. Lights and eights blinking in tandem. I feel for the door handle, pull it, eject myself from the van, lie buckled on the glass pebbled tarmac where I open my eyes to see a night filled with stars.

Sometimes what you think is the sky is only the cold metal roof of a family minivan.

I stand up, wrench the back of the van open. No Paul. I stare through the shattered windshield. Even through foggy thoughts I can do the rudimentary maths. I walk to the front. The van is nestled up against the barrier, front end caved. The car we hit has done a one-eighty, drifted across two lanes. It faces the wrong way, so that at a glance it appears nothing is damaged.

Sheepshank stomach. Half-hitch heart. I know what I'm about to see. My eyes adjust. Paul's body lies prone forty paces past the crash. I stumble over. I'm almost in touching distance when I realise I'm walking in the remnants of his face: blood, bone, bits. I jump to the left.

I'm twenty-two, looking at my best friend's body. *I can't find his face,* I say.

I'm twenty-two. Dad is picking me up from the airport in London. Paul is two days dead. Dad doesn't say much. I went away his boy, came back a stranger. I apologise. He talks about the weather. We're different after this. He couldn't help it. Paul was a person, not a carpet.

Here, now, I sit next to Paul, take his hand, say sorry. I never got the chance last time. I didn't know how to say goodbye, then. I sat, shocked and silent. Tongue-tied. Tearful.

After three days of traversing my own mind, it's not a huge surprise when he rolls over, sits up, takes his hand back. *Stop being a mopey cunt, will you,* he says. *It's not over yet.* He puts his hand back out. *While you're here, smell my fingers.* He laughs, blood dripping all over the sheet.

Traffic starts to stack up behind us. I can't see the cars, the drivers. Only dipped headlights and darkness. A chorus of horns punctuate their own futility. In the distance, sirens. You're never far from a siren in America. Here they echo over the curve of the earth. Closer, an alarm rings between my ears. I'm on the clock. It's day four. I need to keep moving.

Guess this is where you leave me, I say.

It was always going to end here.
You didn't get to see the end.
Another time, maybe.
Another time.

Gurgle.

Cough.

He turns over. Unface down. The way I left him a decade ago.

An ambulance arrives, blue light flashing between orange flickers. Amber and teal. I watch the paramedics lead my twenty-two-year-old self, shocked and shivering, to the back of the truck, a foil blanket wrapped over my shoulders. I look like I've just killed my best friend.

Maybe I killed myself then too. Maybe it just took a decade to realise.

Behind me, a loud bang as the side of the minivan slides open. Jon climbs from the wreckage. Or falls from it, depending who you ask. *Shit*, he says. *Two crashes in two days. You're killing me.* After a beat he adds the word *literally*. He rolls his neck, his shoulders. I hear the pop and crack of air escaping his joints. He asks if Paul is dead again. I nod. *Shit. Guess he's used to it by now.*

Keep moving. I turn heel, stride away from the crash, from the traffic. Jon follows along. A swelling crowd of memories have abandoned their cars in the tail back, deciding to walk rather than get left behind by the plot. A highway full of broken promises on a last-chance mercy drive.

Jon says: *Is a road trip still a road trip if you finish it on foot.*

Sample tweet: *If at fence you don't succeed, buy JoeSeal.*

I hold my notebook, rolled like a baton. It feels heavy, burdensome. I haven't written in days. There is nowhere to put it, no one to hand it off to. Books were a refuge, once. This one feels like a prison. A story I'm trapped in. *Most writing is avoiding writing,* Jon says. *You're doing great.*

After the break-up I couldn't read, couldn't write, couldn't concentrate on much of anything.

The way I got back into reading was I started buying children's books. Books with big print, simple themes. My favourite is *Not Now, Bernard.* It's about a lonely kid who becomes the monster that haunts him. Any book is a self-help book if you read it right.

Smoke billows across the highway from the burning expanse beyond: plains or meadows or small towns. I don't know. The smog, caustic, acrid, has cut visibility to a few feet. I pull my T-shirt over my nose, blink tears from my eyes. Jon ties a bandana around his face. We look like we're about to hold up a gas station. His fuse is running short. He gets bumped and goes full New Jersey. *Hey buddy, I'm walking here.* He turns to me and grins. *Always wanted to say that.*

In the crowd my brother and I barge between bodies, pushing, scuffling, laughing. We used to be so small. We bounced, then. Before life made us big and fragile.

We're seventeen and eighteen, at a gig. An Emo band we both love. It's already packed. I take point, Pete falls in behind, hands on my shoulders. I'm the biggest person there. I wade through the crowd, brushing everyone aside until we're at the front. Pete does the apologies. *Sorry about him. Sorry. Nothing I can do.* We stand side-by-side at the front rail for the rest of the gig, belting every line.

I'm dragging my feet, shuffling. A woman pushes past. I recognise her hair, long, brown. My ex-wife. I call after her, coughing, but she doesn't turn round. The last time we spoke she slapped me, told me to fuck off. When people ask why we broke up, I say we didn't make each other happy. What I don't say is that I made her miserable. What I don't say is there was overlap.

I try to avoid fights. I tell people it's because I'm worried I'll really hurt someone. When I used to fight with my brother, the rage was out of control. I couldn't stop punching. I didn't want to. Like I was made for violence. Now I worry I'll kill someone. Or that I'll want to.

What I'm really worried about is that if someone fought back, I'd lose.

Ash falls from the sky like snow. Black smoke billows in the breeze. Crops still blaze. I catch a glimpse of Sophia in the smog, she's with someone, he has his arm around her. I try to get closer but bodies block my path. My heart is racing. I feel sick. The woman I love and the man she left me for. My body rejects the image. I rush to the barrier, kneel, hurl bile into the blackness below. Finally I spit, stumble away. As I steady myself, the earth starts shaking beneath us, shifting, cracking. The landscape splits apart, all around us the chasms and fissures of a fractured mind.

When it stops, I'm lying on the deck. I can't see Jon. The road remains mostly unscathed, a four-lane salvation passing through the ruin. What a freeway does is it insulates you from reality. Stick to the road, and you can traverse a whole continent without seeing any of it.

Sample tweet: *The best defence is a good fence. Buy JoeSeal.*

When she left, when books didn't work, I quit my job, looked for other ways to fix myself. I tried yoga. I tried jogging. Ate through all my savings. I self-diagnosed my way through the DSM V. I took anti-depressants, crashed off them. I borrowed money from my parents. Maxed out my credit card. I took blue pills, had boring sex with boring people. I masturbated generously. I asked myself: *What would Patrick Swayze do.* Eventually I found drugs.

I started by microdosing LSD. You take amounts so small you don't hallucinate. But you do notice a change in perception. It's a little like trading in your old cathode-ray TV for a 4K flat screen. The image is suddenly richer, sharper. Everything is in HD. Time slows slightly. Light takes on a different quality. It dances on the edge of your vision, fluttering, twinkling.

The road is thick with bodies now, panicked by smoke, by tremors. I'm falling back. I try to speed up but my feet are indifferent, unruly. Someone throws a shoulder. I almost trip over one of those wheeled cases people always drag behind them. A hand on my arm steadies me. *Easy there*, he says. *I've got you.* My dad. He braces my weight, picks up the pace. *I've got you.*

I'm ten, walking home with my dad and brother. We've been to the football. Dad doesn't so much walk as march. We have to jog to keep up. Our pleas to slow a little go unanswered. He hates crowds, so he walks quickly. It's his superpower. That and packing the dishwasher.

Later, when I'm older, a head taller than him, I'll still struggle to keep up.

With my arm around his shoulder we weave through the crowd. Dad navigates stubborn bodies with elbows, threats. Not that he's violent. Scrappy maybe. Never found a fight he backed away from. Especially not when it involves his kids. I once watched him knock out a guy for calling my brother a dickhead. He's mostly silent. This is the closest we've come to a hug in years. *Have you thought about what this will do to your mother*, he says.

I'm twenty-nine, telling Mum I have clinical depression, the kind that doesn't go away. She starts crying, asks if it was her fault. *I don't think it's anyone's fault*, I say. *These things just happen.*

I'm thirty-one and my mum is asking me if I've ever thought about killing myself. I say no.

I tell Dad I'm okay to walk by myself for a bit. By the time I finish the sentence, he's gone.

When my brother was born, Dad planted a tree in our garden. He planted a second when I was born, fifteen feet from the first. The trees grew as we did, always fifteen feet apart. We used them as goal posts. Sometimes a branch would reach too far across the gap, and Dad would cut it back. A few months ago, he had to cut one of the trees down. It was rotten, diseased. He never said which.

My brother isn't a fighter. But he worked out a way to hurt me. Words. He and Paul would taunt me. Small things that stung all the same. They'd tell me I was adopted, that I had no friends. That I was a virgin. The thing about words is that they don't land straight away, the way a punch does. Bruises heal in a day or two. Words linger like unexploded bombs.

I'm not a fighter. Not any more, at least. Unless you count the night I was out with Sophia and punched the guy from her work in his stupid beautiful face.

A thing I used to wonder was what would happen if I punched someone hard enough in the back of the head that my fist broke through their skull, mashed their brains into a pink pulp.

The crowd close ranks as I walk, try to stop me passing. They conspire to ferry and funnel, to kettle, to keep me in place. I overtake an old colleague, a man who spent his life padding around at half pace, ambling, no concept of the space he occupies. The kind of person who is just gratuitously in the way. Even from the other side of a room.

Like an average work-day commute, I oscillate from bemusement to fury, fists balled, shoulders hunched, throwing a *fuck's sake* at every opportunity. Clock's ticking. I don't have time for this. It's only when I've been fighting through them for an hour, maybe more, that I think to look up.

In the distance, a liquid skyline ripples in the breeze. It moves in the air the way a mirage might, shimmering, flickering. A towering cityscape rising from the east coast of my mind. New York. The end. I tumble to the floor on the shoulder of the road, spent. Too exhausted to continue.

The problem with LSD is it's hard to get hold of. Ketamine is easier. So I switched to that.

The sound of hooves on tarmac. A voice. Jon. *Howdy, pilgrim,* he says. *Need a ride.* I turn to see him mounted atop a horse I recognise: Lightning, my trusty steed. It's a long story. *Found him grazing on a patch of grass a mile or so back, scared shitless by the quake, poor guy.* He ruffles Lightning's mane. *We soon calmed you down, though, didn't we.* Jon Bon Jovi, horse whisperer.

It's not that long a story. Lightning is a 16-hand dark bay. The reason he exists is drunken fantasies Paul and I had about riding into battle, smiting enemies. That was a long time ago. It's a good decade since I last shouted, *Lightning, ma trusty steed!* in faux Scots brogue.

Memories are good like that, casually grazing in the pastures till you need them.

Jon pulls me up behind him. He kicks, clicks his tongue. Lightning moseys down the road. I grab Jon's waist. Butch and Sundance ride again. Only in this case, for the first time.

Clip clop. Clip clop.

Eighteen

New Jersey / Violence, Part II

The tunnel yawns, stretches under the river. The one between here and the end. I didn't make it this far last time. I flew out of Newark. Paul's body was on the same flight. Most of him, at least. His face was in a gutter, pressure washed from the highway he died on.

Water runs the road surface slick. Black tarmac ripples, shimmers under fluorescent bulbs. The walls are ceramic tile, glossy. Everything is tinted blue. A tunnel directed by Michael Mann. Jon's at home on horseback. Me, less so. Lightning ambles with a lilting gait. I'm not leaning back. You should always lean back when riding a horse down a slope.

Graffiti scrawled in black marker on the tile: *This is not not an exit.*

Jon hums something by Morricone. I gnaw a plaster on my finger. The webbed fabric frayed where I've picked at it. I bite loose threads, spit them out. The plaster is there because I bit my nail down to the pulp, chewed till I tasted blood, thick and ferric. I have done myself a violence.

My brother and I used to fight, the way most brothers do. Problem was he wouldn't hit me back. I'd hit him, and keep hitting him. I feel bad about it now. I write him texts sometimes. To say sorry. For the times my eyes rolled red with rage. For the times he'd ask if that was all I had and I'd hit him till my fists were sore. I never send them.

A rule we had is we'd never hit each other in the face.

The only time he hit me back he broke my nose.

Ahead, a swell of wrongs surrounds two cars in the middle of the tunnel. Faces I recognise: a girl I dumped by pretending to go to hospital for dialysis, a chap whose girlfriend I used to sext with. My stomach drops. Between the cars, I see who the Many-Faced Man is talking to. Sophia.

Jon kicks us to a trot. *Oh good,* he says. *For a moment there I thought we were out of trouble.*

I'm twelve, punching the wall in my room. I want to make sure my knuckles are lined up properly. I heard that you can break the bones in your hand if you punch wrong. So I practise. I hit the solid brick wall with both fists until I get it right every time. I want to be ready. I'm not sure what for.

In our bubble, we're out at a club. Her colleague tries to pull her away to the bathrooms with the promise of white. I ask her not to. *Don't be a downer,* he says. He grins at me. I tell him his nose is bleeding. He tells me it isn't. I punch him. *It's bleeding now,* I say. The bouncers throw me out. Sophia follows, shouting. I apologise. What I don't tell her is how good it felt.

In tiny block letters on the tile: *Some men just want to watch themselves burn.*

The crowd turns to face us, closing ranks to block my path.

Lightning is anxious, snaking sideways. Jon pulls the reins. *Whoa, boy.* They surge forward. Jon kicks and Lightning rears on command, front legs clearing the first wave of wrongs. We push and trample our way into the mass of bodies, hands grabbing legs and feet, trying to fell us from our mount.

I can see Sophia and the Many-Faced Man standing, centre circle. I dive into the crowd, use my shoulders, elbows to fight through. *Fuck it,* Jon says, leaping out backward. He crowd-surfs a moment, ever cool, before he's pulled down into the mosh pit with the rest of us. I push my way towards Sophia, trip, tumble into three inches of rainwater. I lie at her feet, stunned. Sounds wash together. The water runs red, as if the sky is bleeding. I sit up. The crowd quiets.

What are you doing, she says.
We're here to rescue you, I say.
She sighs. *I don't need rescuing.*
That's not what it looks like to me.
Just stop, she says. *You never listen.*

I see the missile too late, a ball of yellow flame thrown from the crowd. A petrol bomb. It misses us, smashes against the tunnel wall, exploding fire across tile.

Lightning bolts. Wrongs scatter as he bucks and tramples. Others surge towards Jon and me. We stand back-to-back, pushing them off. *Fought our way out of worse,* Jon says. I raise my dukes, breathe heavy. *Let me guess,* I say. *You always wanted to say that.* I try to punch, but my arms are slow, heavy. I have no strength, like my limbs aren't my own, like this is all a bad dream.

Jon says: *Get angry.*

I say: *I don't know how.*

I'm eleven. I fight every day. At home. At school. Any slight sent my way, I'll fly off the handle, throw fists, feet. At lunch I wrestle enemies to the ground. It doesn't matter if I lose. What matters is the fight. Later, when I'm bigger, stronger, my anger will start to scare me. I'll decide to stop fighting before I hurt someone. I'll stop punching walls, stop rising to bait. I'll learn to walk away. But for now I'm a bag of burning rage, barely contained behind bruised skin.

As we fight, the Many-Faced Man climbs into his car. Sophia slides into the passenger seat, avoids my eye. Then I see Fisher, tail wagging in the back seat. They're helping each other. My ex, my bully. She's going to leave. And she's going to take him with her. He steps on the gas.

Sophia's car sits empty. I make a break for it. Jon pulls me back. *Don't,* he says. I spin, swing at him, clip the side of his head. His hat tumbles off. *He's got my dog.* As I turn to run the air ignites in front of me, a wall of flame and glass floors us both with a terrible roar.

We interrupt this broadcast. A high-pitched tone rings out. The picture is all static. My shoulder screams, so does my hip. My palms burn. I can't breathe, can't remember how. Finally, I cough, gasp in a lungful of air. I look up to see the car reduced to a roaring furnace of twisted metal.

Jon rolls over, sloshes for purchase in the puddle. I stand, slowly, help him to his feet. He groans, *Fuck,* picks up his hat, tips out the water. *I'm sorry,* I say. He grabs my shoulder, coughs up a good half a lung. *Well,* he says. *You know what they say. Never beat your heroes.*

The crowd closes in. Another bomb lands nearby, filling the tunnel with fire, smoke. It's a full-scale riot. I cover my mouth. Bottles smash against tile. Where there's smoke there's a sprinkler, only the water spraying from the spigots is red, thick. It covers us like syrup.

A man moves towards us, face obscured, waving a pipe. He points it at me, shouts something I can't hear. *You can stop this,* Jon says. The man raises the bat, swings, misses. *You can stop this.*

I take a deep breath, picture the tunnel. All fire and blood. I've got this. I exhale slowly, see her smiling over the top of a book, snug in one of my T-shirts. The screaming stops. Silence now, save for the trickle of water from the sprinklers. I open my eyes. Wrongs gone, riot over.

A month after the bubble burst she arranged to collect her things. I didn't have much. Some toiletries, a couple of books. I could have met her somewhere, but I didn't. I made her come to me. I don't know what I hoped. A kiss. A fuck. It wasn't that kind of goodbye. It was awkward. She was tense, stilted. She said a few words. Words that hurt. Took her things, turned around, left. I thought it was disinterest. Dislike. I realised later what it was. Fear. She was afraid of me.

I've never hurt her, never would. That wasn't the point. Men like me hurt women all the time. I'd made her come to my flat. Closed the door behind her. Looked at her with lust and longing. I've spent years making myself strong. Lifting weights, punching walls. There's a rage inside me. She's seen it. I'm dangerous, whether I intend to be or not. To her, that day, I was a threat.

In marker on the tile: *One man's romance is another's restraining order.*

Red rear lights disappear into tunnel black. Sophia is gone. Jon squints, stares into an empty flask. *Well, pilgrim,* he says. *Guess we're finishing this thing on foot.*

I say: *Why does she keep leaving.*
He says: *Why do you keep asking her to stay.*

That thing Epstein said: *Insanity is playing the same record over and over and expecting to hear a different song.*

The sound is unmistakable. We're not five paces before we hear it. The bulbs in the section of tunnel ahead are out. Everything is shadow, confusion. *Clip. Clop.* Then from the dark, we see him. I shout: *Lightning, ma trusty steed.* He trots over, blows at us, butts me with his head. I ruffle his mane. Jon rubs his nose, whispers: *Why do you say his name like that. Is he Scottish.*

Jon's arms hang round my waist as we stroll through the tunnel, a distant light growing brighter. We're both leaning forward, the way you should when walking a horse uphill. *What aren't I getting, Jon.* He grins. *The list is long and distinguished,* he says. My mouth curves into a smile.

I'm twelve, convinced someone will arrive in my town looking for a kid that's the best at something, rollerblading, or climbing trees or something, and I'd be that kid and they'd take me off on some grand adventure to save the world, just like in the films I loved. No one ever came.

I'm thirty-two, tired, bored. I just want to sleep. I take the rest of the Ketamine I've been microdosing. The room starts to drift into the distance, like I'm looking through the wrong end of a telescope. I'm that kind of tired where I can't sleep, so I drop a sleeping pill. When that doesn't work, I take another. Then a couple more. Wash them down with whiskey. Finally, eyelids heavy, I drift off.

I have done myself a violence.

Nineteen
New York / Lies

The skyline isn't liquid at all. The buildings here crumble, collapse. Waterfalls of concrete cascade to the ground. From a distance, what shimmered is up close: a city falling apart. And it's beautiful. The scale of it. The way sunlight falls down side streets. The way the moon hangs in the sky, like it has shrugged off the night. It's mid-morning on day five. This is the end.

This isn't the end, Jon says. He tells me to pull up. *We should probably go incognito.* We take plastic sunglasses from a market stall set up on the sidewalk. His are in the shape of stars, mine are hearts. He gives me the thumbs up. *There,* he says. *They'll never see us coming.*

In this New York, bodegas sit next to minimarts. Launderettes and cafes I can see from my window in London rub up against diners and bars and pharmacies. Traffic lights conduct empty streets. Pigeons pigeon. I feel tired. Exhausted. Weak. My head hangs heavy, sleepy. Lightning needs water. *I need to find her,* I say. Lightning snorts. Listen. Laughter on the wind. A child's laugh. *What we need to do,* says Jon, *is find where you've put the end.* He looks over both shoulders, pushes his glasses up his nose. *And stay vigilant. This city'll lie to you.*

A billboard above us shows my body, blue, swollen. It reads: *You're too late.*

I'm nine, learning what suicide is. A neighbour shot himself with a pistol he kept from the war. Mum says he was sad. I ask her what about. *Everything, I suppose,* she says.

I'm fifteen. A girl in our class has slashed her wrists. Everyone says she cut the wrong way, that you're supposed to go with the vein. Curious, I try it in maths class with the point of a compass. I don't get very far, hurts like shit. I decide if I ever kill myself I don't want it to hurt.

That thing you read about lethal injections. They use three drugs. The first shuts down the lungs. It's all they need, really. The second and third are overkill. Three deaths for the price of one.

I say: *Shouldn't you know where the end is.*
Jon say: *Not if you don't want me to, ace.*

The end should feel both surprising and inevitable. I know this because Jon keeps telling me. *Come on,* he says. *Where would you put an ending in a city like this.* The first place I think to look is the New York Public Library. Even though I've never been I feel like I know it, I've seen it in those pictures everyone always shares. Jon nods. *Seems like the kind of thing you'd do.*

This is a city stitched together from a thousand photographs. From maps I studied on my road trip. From TV and movies. From the lyrics of songs. Knowledge I've never had chance to contextualise. I don't know how most of it fits together, but I know that the Lincoln tunnel drops us on 10th Avenue. I know that Central Park is pretty much central, that Times Square starts at West 42nd Street. And I know the general aesthetic. How wide the avenues are. What the buildings look like. The columns and cornices. I know the stoops and sidewalks, the steam vents. The classic yellow cabs. The fire escapes.

I know I'd have fallen in love with it, given a chance.

The city I've conjured is a dream. *Vanilla Sky* empty, disintegrating fast. The streets are littered with glass and stone, cars covered in concrete dust. At Bryant Park we dismount. Take stock. *Time's almost up, chief,* Jon says. *You feel it.* I nod. It's like I'm falling slowly asleep.

Lightning drinks from the fountain. Jon stretches. I find Sophia sitting on the library steps, head in hands. *This isn't the end, then,* I say. She shakes her head. *He took Fisher,* she says. *I'm sorry.* I park myself next to her, pistons creaking. I tell her not to worry. *You shouldn't listen to him,* she says. *He thinks he can do a better job of being you. But he's not you.* I pick at a hole in my Cons. *He's the voice I hear when I close my eyes,* I say. *He's every doubt. Every failure, every defeat.*

You can't let him win, she says.
I won't, I say. *Promise.*

She's tired too, fading. I see it in her eyes. *What is it you pine for,* she says. *We weren't perfect.* I kick at a step. *I love you,* I say. *It doesn't have to be perfect.* I look at her now, try not to lose myself. She holds my eye a moment. *I wish I could believe you,* she says.

The first time I told her I loved her, she asked me to tell her again. She smiled, glassy-eyed, as I repeated the words. *I love you,* she said. *I love you.* Better men have melted for less.

Perhaps we have to finish this thing together, I say. I stand, offer to help her up. *I tried to tell you that on the train,* she says. She climbs to her feet unaided. *I know,* I say. *I wasn't ready to listen.* I put my hand out again. *I am now.* She thinks about it. *You're such a tote bag,* she says.

We slap hands, bump our fists, flip each other off. A handshake we used to share in secret.

In our bubble we talked about kids. What it would be like. Afternoon picnics in the park, our daughter walking between us, hair braided like her mother's. Maybe I did all the talking. Maybe it was me who believed it, who bought every line. Tell a lie long enough it starts telling itself.

A cough. Jon. *What's the play, chief.* A column collapses, crashes down the stairs beside us. Then we hear the motorbikes. Exhausts echo through stereo streets. *We need to find that ending,* Jon says. I take the stairs two at a time. *We'll find it,* I say. *But I need you to buy us some time.*

He removes his starburst sunglasses. *You want me to give them the ol' run around,* he says. He throws me a serious stare. *It would be my goddamn pleasure.* He skips giddily towards Lightning, climbs into the saddle. He might be a figment of my imagination, but he lives for this shit.

Once I find the end, you'll know. I say.
Yeah and so will he, Jon says.
I'm counting on it.

He puts his sunglasses back on. I thank him. *Hey,* he says. *I'm your Huckleberry.* He keeps saying that. *I don't think that means what you think it means*, I say, but he's not listening. He belts out a *yee haw*, tugs at the reins, and they gallop away. So much for stealth.

Sophia takes point. *Any bright ideas*, she says. I flip through the buildings I know in the city. *Maybe*, I say. *Just one. Head east.* She's faster than I am. Tired legs don't carry quick enough.

The street is a gauntlet lined with cliffs of glass. Panes peel from their frames, shattering around us. We weave as we walk, taking refuge under awnings. The motorbikes sound like they're everywhere at once. On top of us, a mile away. She takes my hand, picks up the pace.

I read that walking is just your body stopping itself falling over.

She once said talking to me is like talking to Google.

As a kid, I always wanted a thing. Some kids broke bones, got a cast. Some kids wore glasses. Some were great at football, or maths. I didn't have a thing. I never broke a bone, never got a cast or crutches. I wanted a thing so badly I pretended to be deaf for a week or so.

Later, the thing I got was major depression.

Or, you know, the absence of a thing.

Ahead, I see the arched windows of Grand Central Terminal. St Paul's Cathedral sits across the street. I'm pretty sure that's not supposed to be there. I'm wheezing, panting. She takes my arm. *Come on.* My eyes fall on her and I'm lost again. I still have the pain. It's the poetry I miss.

The slightness of her upper arm. The breath-taking angles of her shoulder. The slow curve of her neck. The crease in her stomach where the skin pinches when she sits. The fuzz around her nipples. Her ribs, the peaks and troughs of bone under soft flesh. The moles, the pimples.

She was poetry to me. Every part of her. She still is.

Depending how your depression manifests you might have co-morbid conditions. Bonus disorders thrown in free of charge: Anxiety, insomnia, OCD.

Co-morbid. People can be like that. Each a symptom of the other.

Sophia helps me through the door, shuts it behind us. Outside, the sound of idling engines; inside, our footsteps echo on stone. I've seen the ceiling mural, the constellations, in pictures. Here, I look up to find a swirling galaxy. Greens, reds, arms extending in a spiral.

We climb the steps at the end of the concourse, where the Oyster Bar would be. Instead we find auditorium seats, ripped from a theatre we once visited in London. I don't recall the play. We were pretty drunk. We sit, slouch in our seats, stare at an empty station. Engines grow distant.

This isn't the end then, she says. I shake my head. *What happens if they catch us.* I look at the clock. Four minutes to midnight. Not the actual time. It's a warning. It ticks over as I watch. Three minutes now. *Can't be anything good*, I say.

In our bubble we're walking home from a bar. She lights a cigarette. Sometimes I'll take it from her, steal a drag, hand it back. But now I just watch. She inhales, blows blue smoke through pursed lips. Suicide in slow motion. It's beautiful.

Remember when you saw Leonard Cohen, I say.
She laughs. *Never gonna let that go, are you.*

In our bubble we took the day off, booked a karaoke booth. Got roaring drunk. After, we're stumbling around Soho in search of cigarettes and mischief when she thinks she spots noted Canadian singer-songwriter Leonard Cohen in line at Starbucks. She's determined to say hello. She's also five gins deep on an empty stomach. The man who might be Leonard Cohen orders something fluffy, the kind of coffee people who hate coffee drink. He turns around, waves at a woman who might be his wife. It's clearly not noted Canadian singer-songwriter Leonard Cohen. I doubt Len drinks anything fluffy. Seems more of a black and bitter kinda guy. *That's definitely him*, I say. *Quick*. She nods, trots over, introduces herself. When she returns she hands me a coffee, frowns, slurs. *Wasn't him*. The man who might have been Leonard Cohen walks by, tips his hat, apologises again for not being noted Canadian singer-songwriter Leonard Cohen. *Hallelujah*, I say, and Sophia spits flat white all over the pavement.

Later, my mouth on her cunt, I hum 'Hallelujah' as she writhes, giggles, tells me I'm out of tune. I laugh, try 'Famous Blue Raincoat' instead. I hold her hip bones, keep her still, slowly roll my tongue over her clit, let my fingers slide inside her until her orgasm soaks us both.

Here, now, I ruin the moment by telling her I miss making her come.

You can't help it, can you, she says.
And what, you never think about it, I say.
Of course I do, but it's not all I think about.

We fall silent again. I know she thinks about me. She sent me a text once, a month or so after we broke up. *I can't stop thinking about fucking you.* A low moment. It didn't go anywhere. She apologised straight after, continued seeing him. But I know I'm still in her head too, somewhere.

The clock ticks over. Something clicks. A thought, an idea. A decision. *I know where it ends,* I say. I stand, start to move, feeling buoyed, newly energised. She follows behind. *We have to be quick,* I say. *Now I know, he knows too.*

On the concourse, light falls through the windows in great columns, the way it did in old photos I've seen. The way it can't any more. Nowadays, skyscrapers built around the terminal block out the sun. We ruin all the best things. At least here I can see it the way it should be.

I try to lighten the mood. Sophia tells everyone her first album was Elliot Smith, but that isn't true. It was Roxette. I laugh. *What,* she says. I shake my head, smiling. The thought catches up to her. *I hate you,* she says. She makes an angry face and I sing a bar of 'The Look'.

I'm eleven, running away from home. I walk into the woods, climb a tall tree, sit there a while. I decide I'll build a treehouse. Forage from the land. Then darkness arrives. I'm cold, hungry. I get home late and Mum asks where I've been. I blame the tree. I blame the night. It's not lying if you're trying to spare someone's feelings. Truth is just the lies you choose to believe.

When she broke up with me I did what I do best. I ran. I quit my job, threw myself into casual flings, tried to flush her from my mind. It didn't work. I didn't work. I couldn't get hard for anyone else. Sometimes, if I closed my eyes, focused, felt their legs tense around my face, I could convince myself they were her. For a little while at least. Just enough erection to perform.

At the door, we stop to check the coast is clear. *The thing that really pisses me off*, she says, *is that you think it was a lie. I did love you. And I meant all the things I said. About us. About family. You're fun and funny and kind. But you left no room for me. I didn't leave because I didn't love you. I left because I needed to look after myself. I couldn't do that with you.*

I say: *I loved you. I love you.*
She says: *Then believe me.*

A billboard sells Occam's Brand Razors: *The simplest shave is usually the right one.*

I'm thirty-two, lying on the floor of my one-room flat. Breath slow, vision blurred. I'm scared. Ketamine makes the lights dance. It feels like I'm falling asleep. If I survive this, I'll tell them it was an accident. *I'm sorry*, I'll say. *I was trying to fix myself.* It'll sound better. But I'm tired. It's time.

The final two things she told me. *I love you* and *I can't do this any more.* She meant both.

On a billboard across the terminal: *We will misremember it for you, wholesale.*

I said the last time I saw Sophia was two weeks ago, but that isn't true.

The last time I saw Sophia, she told me she was pregnant.

Twenty

New York / Lies, Part II

There is a sun setting, somewhere. I get the sense this is the last one. The city is caught in the endless afternoon of autumn. Blue skies, cool breeze. Twenty-two degrees. I can barely stand. She's fading too. We walk, half cut in the dusk light, amid a tapestry of brick ruin. Chunks of city crash down around us. Dereliction plays in surround sound. More Bang than Olufsen. The stuttering subconscious of a faltering life. It's a mess. If you wait long enough everything falls apart.

Above us, billboards hang from every wall. Some of the billboards have billboards. Several show my face, camera angled down, carefully positioned to highlight my cheekbones, downplay my double chin. Sophia is unimpressed. *You're more handsome when you don't try so hard.*

On a billboard: *You're a joke.*

The second time I saw her she was fifty pixels tall. An avatar. She was all smiles, eyes shining under curls of golden hair. She was away for work, so we talked over text in the days after the kiss. We messaged until two or three in the morning, woke up together, slept together. Sexted.

She was always worried I'd fallen in love with an idea. An image. One I could project my desires on to. I always told her I hadn't. And yet here she is. An avatar. Her words, most of them, are her own. Things she's told me. But her actions, her desire to leave, they're mine. I can give her the autonomy, the will to be rid of me. But the game is artifice. I'm playing myself.

I know this isn't real, I say. *But can I kiss you.* She looks at me with all the affection and nostalgia I can give her. *Even if it isn't true*, she says. I nod. *Lie to me*, I say. She steps forward, leans in. Her lips are so soft. I run my fingers over them, rest my forehead against hers.

As we part, a shower of meteors burns in the upper atmosphere. Hundreds of them, thousands, flaring in slow motion across the sky. Leonids. *The end is nigh*, she says. I shrug. *An apocalypse isn't the end of the world.* She laughs, half humouring a bad joke. I'm only half joking.

Ahead is where this all ends. The Chrysler Building. A silhouette stands sentry outside, a faceless black shape betrayed by his form. He steps from the shadows, features restless, ever shifting. All of them mine. The Many-Faced Me. He's flanked by the riders we ran from earlier.

He doesn't need to introduce them. I know who they are: Shame, Doubt, Embarrassment, Guilt.

Also, their names are written on their shirts.

Look at you, he says. *Slumming with the slut. She's made you weak.* She goes for him. I pull her back. He chuckles, looks at me. *That cunt ruined your life, and you're going to help her leave.* Behind him, I spot Fisher locked in the revolving door.

Every time he speaks, Shame, Doubt, Embarrassment and Guilt repeat things he says. *Cunt, joke, pathetic.* They laugh and spit and do their best to intimidate us. He steps out of the way as a chunk of stone lands where he stood. *You're not going to survive this, you know,* he says.

That thing your therapist said: *Don't listen to the bullies.*

I start towards the door. The horsemen step forward, brandishing baseball bats. *That's not a good idea,* he says. He takes a bat from Shame, weighs it in his hands, swings at a chunk of falling stone. *You used to be somebody,* he says. *You blew it, you really fucked it up.*

He takes an apple from his pocket, bites into it, chews loudly. *I could have left already,* he says. *I have the key. That's all I need.* I flinch at the wet smack of the apple in his mouth. Enthusiastic masticators are my Kryptonite. *But I didn't want to miss this,* he says. He spits as he speaks, wiping his many chins with the back of his hand. *I wanted to see the look on your face.*

I say: *That's not why you haven't left.*
I say: *Tell her the real reason.*

The Many-Faced Man looks behind me. *I see you,* he says. *Sneaky little shit.* We turn to see ten-year-old me hiding behind a car. He steps out, slowly, wielding a plastic sword. He raises it up, points it at The Many-Faced Man's many faces. All of them are laughing.

Hey, cry baby, the Many-Faced Man says, *you still wetting the bed. I can smell you from here.*

Shut up, I say.

Everyone knows you piss yourself, he says. *Everyone knows you're weak. Pathetic.*

Shut up.

Look at what you turn into, look at this fat fuck. Can't even a get hard-on.

Shut up.

Depressed, divorced. You've got so much to look forward to.

Shut up.

I'm surprised you didn't try to top yourself sooner.

Shut your fucking mouth.

He's laughing again. Sophia holds younger me, hands over his ears. *Okay,* I say. *I'll tell her. The key won't work for him. That's why he's still here.* He waves it off. *I'm bored of this,* he says.

I don't let it go. *It won't work for him because he's a fraud,* I say. *I mean, you said it. He's a part of me, but he's not me. He's just the bad stuff. The dregs.* I turn my back to him. *What he doesn't know is the key won't work for me either. It's your key. The dumbest thing he did was ditch you. You're the only one Fisher will let in. Great judge of character, that dog. And a very good boy.*

Enough, the Many-Faced Man says. *Bring her to me still breathing.* Shame and Embarrassment flank us from one side,

Doubt and Guilt from the other. Sophia stands in front of younger me, I stand in front of her, brace myself. Doubt swings his bat high. This is going to hurt.

He's about to strike when we hear it. Hooves. Thundering footfall echoes through the streets. Closer now. The henchmen look confused, scared. Then: *Yeah-hooo.* Jon rides from the shadows, kicks Doubt to the ground. The others swing round, ready to lunge at him, but Jon has back up.

Four anthropomorphic dogs – armour clad, riding mechanised horses – follow him into battle. The Tomorrow Knights. They make short work of Shame, Embarrassment, and Guilt. *Pow, zap, crash.* The Knights rope the four fallen henchmen like steer, drag them away. *For a better tomorrow*, younger me says. Sir Blake gives him the thumbs up as he rides away.

Jon, lit golden by the setting sun, majestic, cool, shouts down to me: *You're all clear, kid.*

What are you going to do, Many-Faced Me says. *Cry on me. You're weak. Pathetic.* I think of my dad. *Nobody calls my son a dickhead.* He's stalling, trying to back away. *Enough*, I say.

For the first time in for ever, I find the words. *Look at this kid, just look at him, he's brave, and curious, and interesting, and his imagination, he can do anything, anything, he laughs and he cries and he gets excited, and he's good, he's so good and kind and so much better than me, so much better than you, and he deserves better than your lies in his head, in his ear, tearing him down, telling him he's less, making him feel bad for feeling, for being himself, for being human, and he's so fucking good, so full of light and joy and mistakes and potential, don't you see, how I've listened to your lies and how*

I've been crushed, and how I've been afraid, but he's not afraid of you. I won't let him be. He's better than us. He's better than me. He deserves better.

The next thing I feel are arms around my chest. Jon drags me off myself. The Many-Faced Me lies flat on his back, his faces, all of them, bloody, beaten. I'm shaking, crying. Furious. My fists are clenched, cut up. I used to practise punching walls, to make sure I hit straight. Just in case. Now I know what for. I collapse into Jon, my body convulsing with shuddering, fitting sobs.

Hey, Jon says. *It's okay, buddy. We're okay.*

I take a few stuttered breaths, feel hot tears on my cheeks. A small hand grips mine. Ten-year-old me. He takes a Tomorrow Knight from his pocket, wraps my swollen hand around it. It's Sir Blake. His favourite. He gives me a thumbs-up. I break again, burying my face in Jon's shoulder, entirely undone by the boy I used to be.

Nearby, Fisher whines. He doesn't like it when I'm sad. *It's okay, boy,* I say. I let go of Jon, push open the revolving door. I kneel down, let Fisher lick the salt from my face. *Good boy,* I say, stroking his head, slowing my breathing. *Good boy.*

That thing you read about dogs being good for stress.

I'm expecting a spin off, Jon says. *How does* The Adventures of Lightning Jack *sound.* Sophia walks over, gives Lightning a nose rub. *Shall we,* she says. Jon pats my back with vigour. *I ask for surprising and inevitable, and you choose the Chrysler building.* I nod, wipe my eyes. *Haven't you seen any films,* I say. *Everything always ends at the Chrysler Building.*

Sometimes I get so sad I think I might burst. It's overwhelming. Like fireworks in my chest. Like I'm filled with an infinite sadness, one I can't contain. It comes out in words, in tears. And it's beautiful. Sometimes I wonder if this is how other people feel with happiness. Full. Alive.

When I turn around, the Many-Faced Man is gone. For now at least.

That's all you can do with bad thoughts, keep them at bay.

They never disappear for long.

Twenty-One
Tower / Betrayal

The end happens in a tower that looks a lot like the Chrysler Building, an art deco skyscraper raining white stone and steel around us. Even though I've never been, it's my favourite building in New York, partly because of the architecture, partly because of a bit of genius misdirection.

During construction, the Chrysler was competing with 40 Wall Street for the title of world's tallest building. 40 Wall Street's architect increased the height of his tower, began bragging to the press about claiming the world record. But Chrysler architect William Van Alen had a trump card: a secret 125-foot spire built inside the rising frame of his building. It was hoisted into place right at the end of the build, making the Chrysler the world's tallest building by some distance.

It's not even the ingenuity, the sheer elegance of the solution that I love most. It's the *schadenfreude* of it all. The lengths Van Alen went to just to wipe the smirk from his rival's face.

The end hasn't happened yet, but it will. Younger me races off to find other missions, other mischief. I was never great at goodbyes. Jon lets Lightning loose. *Go on, boy*, he says. Lightning brays, trots off happily. He'll be ready next time we need him. *You know what I miss*, Jon says. *Those bits they used to put at the end of films to tell you what the characters did next.*

Fisher pants happily at Sophia's feet, waiting for a command. I look up at the building, raining render and rubble around us. A trick of mind makes the whole thing appear to fall forward. An optical illusion. I close my eyes before I make it happen, before curiosity fells the Chrysler.

The lobby of this Chrysler is something out of *Gatsby*, gilded, gold, sparkling marble. Or it was. My mind paints it monochrome, desaturating every surface save ourselves, the opulent space still stunning in high contrast black and white. I like monochrome. It adds drama, depth.

We hit the button for the lift and the doors slide open. *I don't know what's waiting up there,* Jon says. *But it won't be sunshine and puppies. This is gonna hurt.* Sophia takes my hand. *We'll do it together,* she says. I take Jon's hand. *Together.* We step in and the doors close behind us.

The buttons inside the lift show seventy-eight floors. The Chrysler only has seventy-seven. I hit seventy-eight. Nothing happens. I try more buttons. Nada. Then a voice on the intercom: *What.* Sophia nudges me, points to a camera in the top corner of the lift. *We have your dog,* she says, pointing to Fisher, who walks around his tail a couple of times and sits. *It's okay, buddy,* I say. Static silence. Crackle.

With a jerk and a shudder we start moving.

Sophia and I were in our bubble for almost eighteen months. That's seventy-seven weeks. I did the maths. Everything falls apart if you wait long enough.

The doors open on the first floor. The night we met. A gig somewhere in Camden. A memory made monochrome. But not her. She glows in glorious Technicolor. I catch her eye across the room. Time stops. Everyone else stands frozen. I start to say something but she puts her finger on my lips, kisses me. And so the bubble begins. She's going to break my heart. I'm going to let her.

Floor two. Week two. The doors slide open on my bed. It's the first time we fuck. We undress each other slowly, our scattered clothes the only colour in the room. Later, we'll fuck on every surface, unrestrained, animal. But we start slow. I kiss her whole body, finally settle between her legs, make her come with my tongue. Moans that echo still. After, she straddles my hips, slides me inside her. I keep my feet on the floor for better leverage. The lift doors close on us rolling our hips together. We laugh and kiss like we're not going to tear each other apart.

She says: *Stop this.*
I say: *I'm trying.*

Floor four: We're driving to the coast for a dirty weekend when I start telling her exactly what I'm going to do when we get there. She lifts her skirt, slides her hand into her tights, spreads her knees wide, arm shaking as she rubs her clit. She take her fingers from her knickers, slides them into my mouth so I can taste her. It's dark out and she flickers in the strobing street lights. I keep my eyes on the road, her hand a blur on the periphery. She pushes her hips out of the seat, comes with a sharp breath, a long *fuck*.

Floor eight: We're eating breakfast in bed. She's reading the paper, toast in mouth, wearing one of my dress shirts. It's too much. I put my coffee down, disappear under the duvet. She starts to object, something about eating, and I say, *Me too.* I kiss her thighs, trace my thumb over the thin cotton. She pushes her hips forward, parts her legs. I pull her knickers to the side, draw my tongue over her clit with a long slow stroke. Her plate falls from her hand. A piece of toast lies butter side down on the duvet. She tenses her legs, groans. In the lift, Sophia turns away.

A voice on the intercom, grizzled, faint: *You have to watch.* The door stays open. The sound of the Sophia out in the room coming is difficult to ignore. *They won't close until you watch,* the intercom says. Sophia raises her hands to her face, exhales in frustration. She turns back, watches herself shuddering on the bed, legs locked, hips bucking, *Fuck, fuck, fuck.* The doors close.

Jon places his hat over the camera. The intercom starts to say something but I dig my fingers in behind the panel, wrench it open, rip out the wires. The lift whirrs upwards. *Who is it,* she says. Jon starts to stumble his way through an answer. *I think we all know that it's me,* I say.

Floor seventeen: We're fighting. She slams a door. I punch a wall. She's always been flirty. I've always been jealous. She says she needs trust. *I love you,* I say. It isn't enough.

Floor twenty-four: She's burying her face into the mattress, arse in the air. I'm kneeling behind her, hands clamped to her hips. Our thrusting has shifted the bed out from the wall a good three or four feet. She feels me start to swell inside her. *Come for me, baby,* she says. *I want all of it.*

Sex is rarely this smooth. It's never quite what you remember. You tend to leave out things that don't fit. The unsatisfied thrusts, the pained expressions, the misplaced elbows. That bit at the end where you roll to opposite sides of the bed and finish yourselves off.

The silences between floors grow longer, more despondent. We each of us take a deep breath when the car stops. The higher we go the scenes become more fraught, more desperate, more intense. Jon tries to stay calm. He plays with his lighter, flipping the lid open, closed, open.

Floor thirty-one: We're in bed watching old Tomorrow Knights episodes on YouTube.

Floor thirty-nine: She's sucking my cock in a bathroom stall at a gig, sweaty, urgent, high.

She says: *Is this all I was to you.*
She says: *You never respected me.*

These scenes don't represent us. Not everything we were. Memory doesn't work like that. Eighteen months together, and all I have are fragments. You can't remember everything. You choose a few moments, cling to them. Memories are just postcards you keep sending yourself.

We're in here somewhere, five minutes either side of these scenes.

Floor fifty: The first time she broke up with me. We hold each other, sobbing. The doors close.

The mechanical whir of the lift the only sound preventing silence. And then, a song. My voice is low, clear. Fisher's ears prick up. I sound out the opening lyrics to 'Bed of Roses'. Jon taps out a beat with his foot. He puts his arm around my shoulders, pulls me close, joins in. His voice is richer than mine, stronger. Singing with him gives me chills. He beckons her over, swaying as we hit the part about blondes, nightmares. The look on her face says, *Are you fucking kidding me.*

Floor sixty-one: Sophia and I are fucking in my shower, her legs around my hips, back pressed against the tile. She grabs a handful of my hair as I thrust into her, water draped, insatiable.

Floor sixty-three: Our second break-up. She rolls over to my side of the bed after a sleepless night, starts to back herself into me. Black-and-white bodies on a bright red duvet.

In the lift we sing at the top of our lungs, do our best to ignore the scene. Sophia turns to us, takes a deep breath, and closes her eyes. She joins us on the chorus. She has a great voice. I didn't know she knew the lyrics. We lean back in unison and belt it out together.

Floor sixty-eight: We're in bed, backs against the current mood, being borne apart by sadness.

Fisher, still lying at my feet, jumps up and barks as we hit the final chorus. As the song comes to an end Jon pulls us both close, heads resting together, where we whisper the final lines.

Floor seventy-seven. We're too busy smiling and hugging to notice the scene unfolding outside. I stop when I see it. Grin gone. My bedroom. It's late. We've been up listening to music, talking. We've dozed off. It's the middle of the summer. I've kicked off the duvet. Her head is nestled into my chest. Our legs stretch out, her knee overlapping mine. We breathe in unison.

Two bodies occupying one space. Co-morbid. Alloys. Faint sounds from the speakers. It's peaceful. Our last night together. A week before I get the text. But here, there, on floor seventy-seven, in that bed, we're the best we ever were. I see myself stir awake, stroke her hair, smile. She wriggles a little, lets out a half moan, holds me tighter. I let my eyes close, drift away into bliss.

Sophia is standing next to me. She rests her head on my shoulder as we watch ourselves sleep. *We never managed that for long,* she says. I shake my head. I'd get too hot or start snoring. We'd move to opposite sides of the bed. I'd wake to her pale shoulder rolling away from me.

That's the thing about memory. Those few minutes of sleep can last for ever.

We begin the slow crawl to the final floor, to meet whatever version of me dwells there.

Sorry about the singing, I say. *I didn't know what else to do.* She smiles. *I miss going to karaoke with you,* she says. It's my sentiment, not hers. It makes me feel better anyway. Her hair is pulled back into a ponytail. It's difficult to ignore the soft skin of her neck, the curve of her tits under her T-shirt, the way they rise and fall as she breathes. I smile back. Pretend I'm not lost. *Me too.*

Floor seventy-eight. We don't stop. Fisher barks. *It's okay, boy,* I say. I didn't know he could count. Jon has his lighter out again. *Here we go.*

Unknown floor: My bedroom, must be a few days after the break-up. I'm in bed, trying to sleep, phone in my hand. Face lit by the bright blue glow of the screen. I check to see if she's online. A green dot appears by her name, then goes again. No messages. I keep scrolling, waiting.

Unknown floor: Sophia's flat. There's a man with her, entirely in silhouette. They cast off their clothes, desperate, clawing. She gives him the look I used to get. She's glowing but not for me.

The doors close. She tells me that never happened. *Not to you,* I say.

Unknown floor: I'm flicking through pictures she sent me, desperately wanking to sentiments long since revoked. I've come four times today, and can't stop myself. It's the only way to get dopamine into my system. A few days after this she asks me to delete everything she sent me.

Unknown floor: I see her at a gig. I down the drink I'm holding, order another. Our eyes lock across the room. She looks away first. I see the silhouette walking towards her and I leave, stumble out in a haze of anxiety. I can't watch this. They stand there, laughing at me.

In the lift, my eyes fill with tears. *We never laughed at you,* she says. *We never talked about you.* The doors close. *It doesn't matter,* I say. *There's nothing you could do as bad as I did to myself.*

Unknown floor: Therapy with Emily. *I feel stupid,* I say. *For daring to hope it would end any differently than it did.* She tells me to focus on how we'd found each other. To remember how good it was. *You don't dare to hope,* she says. *Hope is default. Hope can't help itself.*

Unknown floor: She's on my doorstep. The one time she caved, came to see me. We kiss, fumble with our clothes in the hallway, fuck in my bed. It's quick, tempered by guilt, by grief. *Just make me come*, she says. It's not a Richard Curtis script. She leaves soon after. Makes her excuses. *I'm sorry*, she says, slipping out. It's maybe a month after she ended things. It's the last time we fuck.

What I did next was I hounded her. I sent too many texts, called her at all hours, turned up at her flat. Unwilling to let her go, again. *I'm sorry*, I say. *I was out of order*. She says sorry too. *For that. For everything*. We tore so many chunks out of each other we ran out of chunks to tear.

Unknown floor: A week ago. Lunch with Sophia. I wear the kind of blazer she once told me I looked handsome in. For an hour I'm my best self, witty, engaging. She laughs the way she used to. Then there's a long pause. She tells me she's pregnant. I do the maths. It isn't mine. It can't be.

I wanted you to hear it from me, she says. She watches as words, softly spoken, crush completely. I smile, glassy-eyed. *I'm really happy for you*, I say. And I mean it. That's the thing about loving someone. You want them to be happy, even if it utterly destroys you.

Finally, floor seventy-eight. The doors reveal a hallway. Dark, muted, the hum and click of a single fluorescent light, blinking. There is only one door. I recognise it immediately. My flat, back in London. Silver number 9 still screwed to the front. A camera watches us approach.

I've got a sad feeling about this, Jon says.

As I raise my hand to knock, the door creaks open.

Twenty-Two
Tower / Betrayal, Part II

My flat is much how I left it, only darker. Dirtier. More plates piled in the sink, more dust. This version of me sits in my armchair, emaciated, grey. My depression. *I'd offer you a seat*, he says. *But there's only one.* He coughs quite violently. *You look like—* Jon says. He doesn't finish, something stops him mid-sentence. Sophia too. They stand perfectly still, statues, mannequins.

What did you do to them, I say. Fisher sniffs at their legs. *It's my show*, he says. *I can make them do whatever I want*, he says. Sophia's hands reach between her legs. *Stop*, I say. He laughs. It's only now I see the porn playing on the wall behind me. Past lays replayed, projected in widescreen.

He says: *What's worse, that you can't stop thinking about her, or that she never thinks about you.*

I'm thirty-two, sitting in that chair, in this flat. The neighbours are fucking again. They fuck a lot. Either that, or they move a lot of furniture. I haven't had sex in months. I mostly eat junk, watch movies, masturbate. Hoping she'll text. She doesn't. If I press my ear to the wall I can make out sounds. Mattress springs flexing. Occasional groans. When I hear them start I rush to the wall, unbuttoning my jeans, trying to get myself hard, straining to decipher shuffles, squeaks.

Sometimes they aren't fucking. They have heavy feet. I hear them laugh or talk, muted tones, sans context. Cooking, chilling. Those times I just listen a while. They sound happy.

Sometimes they are fucking. Nothing says misery quite like wanking to the sound of strangers fucking. Nothing says loneliness quite like coveting the lives of neighbours you can't see. Nothing says despair quite like learning you can still come without a hard-on.

What Emily said: *If you could talk to your depression, what would you say.*

Here, now, I say: *I thought you'd be taller.*

I feel stupid standing. I sit on the edge of the bed, where I also feel stupid. I rarely had guests over to this flat, none that needed a chair. Fisher brings me his toy, a small stuffed dog he's chewed to pieces. If you really want to fuck something up, love it as hard as you can.

It's time to let her go, I say. He snort laughs. *She told you she was stuck,* he says. *Waiting for a train. She wasn't. She's found her way here half a dozen times over the past year, she's been this close. And each time, we reset. Send her back. And she starts her quest again.* He watches her on the wall. Sex Sophia and I had a long time ago. She comes through cheap speakers. I ask him why. *You know the best way to stop a revolution,* he says. *Let them think they're winning.*

I punch the wall. My fist goes through the plasterboard. I'm not a kid any more. I'm big enough to break things, to do damage.

I'm thirty-two, bringing a date home, my first since her. We drink whiskey, listen to something sad she pretends to like. I pretend not to be mad when she finishes all my good bourbon. I kiss her. Nothing stirs. I scatter kisses like carpet bombs across her stomach, reach her cunt, taste her. Commit to my work. Now things are moving. It's twenty minutes before she comes. Tensing, writhing, convulsing. My face is soaked, jaw sore, hard-on gone. She isn't who I want her to be. I want to ask her to leave, to tell her my cock works fine, just for someone else. We lie in the dark, silent, unsatisfied. Then comes the banging. The neighbours are fucking again.

Why didn't Jon tell me, I say. He's not listening. I walk over to the projector, pull the plug. He sighs. *I know you know that's not Jon Bon Jovi,* he says. *But I'm surprised you haven't figured out who it is.* I lean over him in the chair, ask what the fuck he's talking about. *The coolest person you've ever known,* he says. The second he says it I know exactly who he means.

He grabs his laptop, starts flipping between tabs. I grab his wrist to wrest it away, only to stop the second I touch him. He's ice cold. He pulls his arm back. *How long did he say you had.* I'm pacing again. Fisher watches me, hoping this is a game. I hope so too. *Five days at most.*

The me in the chair looks bored. *It's only been an hour,* he says. *Not even. I'm sure it felt longer.* I ask how long I've got. *Who knows,* he says. *Hours are always doing that to you, aren't they.*

I say: *How do I get back. How do I leave.*
He says: *You've made your choice.*
I say: *I've changed my mind.*
He says: *Too late.*

I tell him I don't believe him. This other me. This parasite. Depression distorts everything. It lies to you. *Are you cold.* he says. *Awfully cold in here.* The thing is I am cold. The room is freezing. I take a T-shirt from a drawer, slip it over the ones I'm already wearing.

You can feel it, he says. *Can't you. This is where it ends.*

That thing you read about depression being an inability to see the future.

Strap in, he says. *May as well enjoy it.* His laugh is searing. I look at my friends, frozen, think of how far we've come. That I don't want it to end like this. *You said this is your show,* I say. *Not any more.* The second I decide to wake them, Jon and Sophia snap out of their slumber.

She lunges at him, the me I fear I am, slaps him, hard. He laughs. *Did he tell you about the other girls he texted,* he says. *Did he tell you about them.* Sophia turns and looks at me. *What, you think I don't know,* she says. *I'm not an idiot. There's a reason I don't trust him.*

He looks at me now. *Fine,* he says. *But he didn't tell you about the times you've been here before. Six by my count. So close. And every time he sent you back to the start, made you do it all over again.* Sophia's eyes flood with angry tears. *He could have let you leave a long time ago.*

Is that true, she says.
Depression lies to you, I say.
I'm not asking your depression.

It was subconscious, I say. *I'm sorry.* She looks defeated. *No,* she says. *It wasn't. You didn't want to let me go. You told me as much.* She's shouting now, shaking, furious. *Don't bullshit me, after everything. After all this.* My depression laughs, delighted by the chaos he's causing.

People think having depression means not being able to laugh, but that isn't true. You laugh all the time. The difference is there's no lasting effect. You feel just as empty afterwards.

Jon gives an unsubtle nod. *That certainly sheds light on a few things,* he says. He winks at me. He may as well be pointing. I walk over, grab the string that opens the blinds. My depression cries out. *Don't.* I pull the cord. Sunlight floods through the window, and with it, colour.

My flat sits resplendent, newly illuminated, rendered in a full spectrum of light. Save for one small detail. My depression lies on his back in the middle of the room, where I left myself out in the world. Blue-grey, bloated, just like on the billboard. I look like a stale bread roll.

I tell people my marriage ended because we didn't make each other happy. That's partly true. I was also texting someone I shouldn't have been. She found out. We didn't last long after that.

That thing Emily said about repeating my mistakes. She says it's defensive. I was so scared Sophia would leave I made it happen. Willed it. It was stupid. Driven by fear, insecurity.

That self-destruct button is awfully big and shiny.

Fisher drinks water from an ornate bowl I didn't know I owned. Sophia sits on the edge of the bed, shoulders hunched, crying tired tears. *I wasn't ready,* I say. *I didn't realise then. That thing they say, about letting go of the things you love, they never say how hard it is. How much it hurts.* Tears roll from cheek to chin, mine, hers. *I know,* she says. *And I do care. I feel bad all the time, thinking how lonely you must be.* She wipes tears from her cheeks. *But you hurt me too.*

Sophia knows about my wrongs. And I know that she's with someone else. I've met him. I punched him in the face. What I'll never know is if she left me for him or if they got together later. Some questions can't be answered. Not here. Not by me. This is only half a story.

I look at Jon. *You should say goodbye.* He steps over, wraps her in a big hug, warm and earnest. Something people should know about Jon Bon Jovi is that he gives great hugs.

After the bubble burst, she came to my place to collect her things. I didn't have much. A few toiletries. Some books. But I made it awkward. I want to be better this time. I say goodbye to Fisher, breathe him in, hand her the leash. He barks as she hugs me. I manage not to get hard.

In our bubble, I didn't understand how fragile she was. I didn't realise that she's more brittle, in many ways, than I'll ever be. That she knew, the first time we kissed, that I was going to break her heart. That I would shatter her completely. I made my pain the narrative, ignored hers.

My last letter to her should have been three words: *Look after yourself.*

Door's open, I say. A red exit sign hangs above it. *What about you*, Sophia says, and I realise I know the answer. *This isn't my ending*, I say. *It's yours*, I say. I shove my hands in my pockets, brace myself for a *told you so* that doesn't arrive.

She smiles. *RIP Jeff*, she says. And then she's gone. She doesn't look back.

This time, I don't ask her to stay.

Jon flips through a pile of notebooks stacked on my desk. Black, battered. Moleskine brand. *They're all the same*, he says. *It's just the same page, over and over*. I tell him I couldn't get the opening right. *Start with the weather*, he says. *Some suicide note*.

You knew, didn't you, I say. *That this wasn't my ending.*
Of course, he says. *But I had to let you figure it out for yourself.*

The Chrysler is crumbling around us, a slow-motion strip tease of brick and glass. It won't be here long. Out of the window waterfalls of rock rain on to the street. The once liquid skyline looks pixellated now, broken windows, jagged edges, as if the scene is ripped from a jpeg.

A section of wall falls away. *Guess that's our cue*, he says. *Any bright ideas*. I open the window. He asks what I'm doing. *Good question*, I say. *Is it still a BASE jump if you don't have a parachute*. He smiles. *No idea*, he says. *But it's not suicide if you're trying to fly.*

We climb out on to the upper-most ledge of the unChrysler. The wind whistles in our ears, bullies us flat against the brick. We creep along the ledge to the corner, where the art deco eagles stand watch over the city. Jon takes my hand, leans out over the edge. *Jesus Mary Christmas*, he says.

This is probably a good time to mention I'm not great with heights. Climbing I enjoy, being at the top of something not so much. *End of the road*, he says. He sings it a little. But not in a way that would infringe any copyright.

My second favourite story about the Chrysler is that once William Van Alen had delivered Walter Chrysler the world's tallest inhabitable structure, Chrysler refused to pay his fee. It's a building made entirely of subterfuge and betrayal. And it's beautiful.

The plan as I understand it involves jumping from the building to force me to wake up. You do it in dreams all the time. Fall off things, wake up. *This gonna work*, I say. He shrugs. *No idea.*

There was a playground rumour that if you fall in a dream and hit the ground, you die.

Jon says: *What this presupposes is that you're not already dead.*

We step out, drape our toes over the edge. A Tomorrow Knight toy falls past us, chute deployed, handkerchief canopy catching the air. He lifts slightly on an updraft before he begins to fall again. We watch him float amid the tumbling stone until he drops out of sight.

I close my eyes, lean forward. Jon leans with me. I take his hand. Start to count. Today we go on three. The next time I open my eyes we're airborne, unmoored, falling fast. I twist in the air to face the floor and spread my arms out wide, ready to embrace what comes next.

The ground arrives slowly and then all at once.

Twenty-Three
California / Dreaming, Part II

It's a cool, calm day in my mind and the birds are flying backwards. Above, a ceiling of trees breaks to reveal a solitary cloud. Then a second. They sit static in the sky, tips tinted orange by the setting sun. The light cutting through the canopy is syrupy, thick. It's golden hour.

How we got here is we fell. A hole. Unwhole. Instead of hitting the ground we found only an absence of it, falling beyond the floor into the shadow of the building. We never found the bottom. No ground to hit, nothing to wake me up. We fell for hours in the pitch black, holding hands to stay together, the way otters do. I think Jon slept for part of it.

Then walls, soil, solid rock. Roots running through like arteries. Eventually we slowed enough to grab hold, climbed the curling tendrils like village simpletons off to slay a giant.

We rest some after the climb. Jon pulls me to my feet, peers into the abyss, spits. The abyss spits back. It lands on his boot. He curses, wipes it off with some nearby bracken. We stand where we started, amid unfelled redwoods, other trees besides, between. This is the forest of the mind.

Jon says: *I know you can ascend, and you can descend. But can you ever just scend.*

After a short stroll, we find ourselves standing atop the tree trunk where we met. The one he pissed from. *What now*, I say. In the treeline ahead, some shapeless form moves among the branches. I'm about to ask if he sees it too, but it disappears into shadow.

In the unquiet, a haunting doubt looms, sits like a spectre between us. It towers over me, this thought I can't shake. Menacing, insidious: *Maybe I'm too late.*

It's this way, Jon says. He points in the opposite direction from the way we went before. *If I'd have gone that way in the first place,* I say. *I'd be home by now.* He doesn't reply right away. Adjusts his hat, hocks a loogie into the brush. *Yeah,* he says. *But where's the fun in that.*

Mum and I have a running joke via text. She asks how I am. *There's a monster,* I say. Sometimes it's in the kitchen, sometimes the bathroom, the bus. Depends where I am. Then I say, *It's going to eat me.* A few seconds later I'll get a reply. *Not now, Bernard.* She usually adds a kiss.

That thing you read about forest bathing. How a walk among tall trees reduces depression and anxiety. Reduces stress. Something about the scale of it all. The Japanese have a name for it.

On the wind, a song: *Hush, hush, whisper who dares.*

We walk the length of the fallen trunk, climb down. I see something bright in the undergrowth, bend to pick it up. A Tomorrow Knight, complete with homemade parachute. As we stroll I take time to carefully fold up the handkerchief, reattach one of the strings, ready for his next jump.

I'm thirty-five, at my own book launch. I meet a friend of a friend who tells me she hasn't read the book but she's heard mixed reviews and hopes she doesn't have to meet the author. *Too late*, I say. She glows bright red. When I text her a few days later, she asks me out for an apology drink. I accept.

I'm thirty-six, unlocking the door to our first flat. After a year of seeing each other, Sara and I move in together. Later she'll make me suffer through jazz as we drink prosecco in the bathtub. But right now we kiss at the threshold, collapse into each other, fuck on the bare floor of our new home.

Stars sparkle quietly in draping dusk. There are trees that don't belong here, hidden among redwoods. Oak, pine, silver birch. Trees I've climbed. Trees I've wanted to. Jon whacks at nettles with a stick, asks me what I'm gonna do when I get back. *You know the guys who stand behind rappers*, I say. *The ones whose job it is to shout yeah every now and then.* He nods like he knows. *Anyway they just stand there and shout yeah sometimes. I think I'd be good at that.*

There's a short scar on my arm. The skin is thick, discoloured. How I got it is I fell playing basketball. My arm locked so violently it seized for a week. Later I found I couldn't straighten it fully. Calcium deposits, apparently. After the trauma, my body grew new bone to protect itself.

We see the trees my dad planted when my brother and I were born. I walk between them and find myself, ten-year-old me, in front of a thick wall of white fog. He stands staring at it. What he's doing is trying to work up the courage to walk through, see what's on the other side.

I hand him his Knight. *He made it all the way here,* I say. He smiles. I take his hand and step towards the fog, just to look. His hand is small, soft. Mine, callused, rough, wraps around his. He doesn't seem to mind. Jon arrives, stands next to us, peers into the fog. *Spooky,* he says.

Do you know how it ends yet.
I think so, I say. *We'll see.*
Is it surprising, he says.
I nod. *And inevitable.*

The fog is like a thick cotton up close. Flat, uniform, as if pressed against an invisible glass. It looks more like a cloud, tired of floating, come to rest on the ground. I place my hand flat against it, without pushing. It's cool to the touch. *What do you think,* I ask my younger self. He shrugs. *You're not scared.* He shakes his head. I wasn't scared of much back then.

All you have to do is go through it, Jon says, standing beside me. I ask my younger self what he thinks. He considers it a moment, sizes it up. *We don't have to be home till dark,* he says. *It's not dark yet.* Jon laughs. He has a point. *We can stay a little longer,* I say.

I have stretch marks where I grew too fast. Where the man I was going to be forced the boy I was to grow big, strong. To pretend to the world I am metal and stone. The scars, hidden out of sight on my hips, my back, show just how easily I break. Soft skin, easily torn.

I ask ten-year-old me if he's ever hunted for gold bears. He shakes his head, asks if they're real. *Oh, they're real,* I say. *They only come out at dusk, hide right at the tops of the trees.* I ask him to pick a tree. *It's a perfect night for gold bears,* I say. He runs off, head full of possibility.

I'm forty-two, reading with my daughter. She's four, and it's my turn to put her to bed. I suggest *Not Now, Bernard*. She screws up her face. *Not now, Daddy*, she says. Since we told her that Sara is pregnant again, her favourite book is one about being a big sister. We settle in, read it together.

Jon and I, slow, tired from a long journey, follow behind. He hands me his hip flask. *Last sip*. I take it just to feel warm. It's still twenty-two degrees but feels colder. Maybe it's the wind. He asks how I'm feeling. I'm never sure how to answer that. Do people want to know. I figure he does.

You ever feel like you're wandering around with a wooden nose, I say. *Hoping you'll be a real boy one day*. He stays silent, puts his arm around me. It's what I needed. I thank him for having my back. He shakes his head, shrugs. *I'm your Huckleberry*. I let him have it.

There is V-shaped scar underneath my bottom lip. From that first car crash. The one I don't remember. I don't have to. My skin remembers, carries the scar to prove it.

Maybe that's what depression is, a scar of the mind.

Younger me leads us to an old oak whose branches hang low enough to climb. *Where's your brother*, I say. I rarely climbed trees alone as a kid, even if that's how I remember it. He points to where Jon is standing, only it's not Jon. It's Pete. Eleven years old. The coolest person I've ever known, even when we were kids. *Race you*, he says, sprinting towards the tree. I run with him, only I'm not me any more either. I'm smaller, lighter, happier.
I'm forty-three, in the park with my family. Sara and I walk with our youngest daughter between us, each holding a hand. Her feet, unsteady, careful, step forward slowly. Her older sister

rides her bike nearby. I look up to see Sophia, walking with her kids. We exchange a smile and a nod.

There are a hundred lives I'll never get chance to live. There are choices I've made I can't undo. People I'll never get to meet. Apologies I'll never stumble through. Life is consequences.

I'm ten, climbing a tree in my mind. My brother, a year older, a head taller, climbs next to me, spiralling up opposing sides until the branches become too thin to hold our weight. From here we can see the whole valley. Chimneys. A church spire. The clock tower at the old mill.

The sun has set, the last embers of daylight glow behind distant hills. If we don't leave we'll be late for tea. We don't move. Not yet. Then Pete stands, unzips his fly, urinates from the top of the tree, hot piss splashing off the branches we'll have to climb later. He shouts down. *Look out below.* I stand up, unzip my jeans, join in. We are the lords of our domain, laughing like jesters.

We'll leave soon. Once we're hungry. When we get home, when Mum asks where we've been, we'll blame the night. We'll say it arrived too soon. She won't stay mad at us for long.

We never speak, my brother and me. But I can always find him when I need him. In here.

Out there, Pete still goes to the football every other week with Dad, still struggles to keep up with his pace, no doubt. Mum goes to see him for coffee on a Saturday morning, for a catch up, for gossip. They go for dinner, my parents, my brother and his wife. It's not that they prefer him. It's that

I forced them to take sides. In absence. In abandonment. I chose for them.

Dusk falls. Jon and I sit at the top of the tree, light fading. Above us, bursts of sadness explode like fireworks. *Time to saddle up*, he says. *People to be, places to do.* I take out my notebook, ask for a minute more. He leans back against the trunk, hat pulled over his eyes, a toothpick he whittled resting between his lips. *Suits me*, he says. *Besides, I've no idea how we get down.*

That thing you read about how people can actually die of a broken heart. It's caused by emotional stress. What happens is the ventricles rupture. Your heart literally breaks.

I've had my heart broken five times. There's no scar tissue. The muscle is thin, fragile. Each break bleeds like the first. They never heal, never get easier. The heart does not callus.

A dog is barking in the distant dark. Closer, my heart beats softly, slowly. A choir of leaves rustle around me. It's cold. The T-shirts I'm wearing, four of them, do little to keep me warm. I use the last of the light to make a note in my book. I roll it up, tuck my pen into my pocket. And I wait.

More clouds now. Rain falls in the distance, we watch it move towards us, a swirling crystal column weaving between trees. Millions of droplets dancing on the breeze, shimmering in starlight. It's quite beautiful. You can be profound about anything if you frame it right.

Jon asks what I wrote. My eyes refocus, adjust to the dark.

I'm happy, I say. *I thought this was a good place to end.*

Thank You

My brother, Robin, to whom this book is dedicated. Ta pal.

My agent, Cathryn Summerhayes, for your belief in me and this book.

My editor, Philip Connor, for your insight and wisdom, and to DeAndra Lupu, Charlotte Hutchinson and the team at Unbound for all your hard work.

My parents, Gill and Richard, for your love and support, and for your tireless publicity efforts. My father, Michael, for your enthusiasm and encouragement.

Maggy Van Eijk for the laughter and everything after.

Richard Skinner for your kind words and guidance, and to Anjola Adedayo, Kelly Allen, Alison Feeney-Grant, Giles Fraser, Maria Ghibu, Daniel Grant, Sybil Joko-Smart, Adele Lawson, Alison Marlow, Trisha Sakhlecha, Helen Trevorrow, Kate Vick and Katie Khan for your council and friendship.

All the patrons listed here who made this book possible.

And finally, Jon, for the music.

About the Author

Dan Dalton is a writer and journalist. He lives in north London. *Johnny Ruin* is his first book.

Supporters

Unbound is a new kind of publishing house. Our books are funded directly by readers. This was a very popular idea during the late eighteenth and early nineteenth centuries. Now we have revived it for the internet age. It allows authors to write the books they really want to write and readers to support the books they would most like to see published.

The names listed below are of readers who have pledged their support and made this book happen. If you'd like to join them, visit www.unbound.com.

Anjola Adedayo	Poubelle Bébé	Hannah Bright
Kelly Allen	Charlie Bell	Ryan Broderick
Jessica Amento	Abigail Bergstrom	Max Brodie
Lee Anderson	Katie Birch	Marie Brooks
Annette Apostolakis	Collette Bird	Rachel Brown
Chris Applegate	Mike Bissett	Scott Bryan
Dominic Atkinson	Owen Blacker	Summer Burton
Daniel Awbery	Dianne Blacklock	Tash Busta
Luke Bailey	Heidi Blake	Sian Butcher
David Baker	Christian Böß	James Butlin
Rebecca Baker	Abigail Boswell	Lauren Callaghan
Sybil Baleanu	Jane Bradley	Cecilia Campbell-
Melanie Ball	Lyle Brennan	Westlind
Melissa Bartlett	Miranda Brennan	Sheila & Brian Carney
Abbey Batchelor	Jo Brewer	Georgia Carroll
Emily Bate	Seth Brewer	Nikki Cartwright
Alison Bayne	Chris Bridgland	Declan Cashin

Erin Chack

Jenny Chamberlain

Catherine Chambers

Rosie Chilvers

Tom Chivers

Jake Christie

Louise Christie

Martin Christie

Nicci Cloke

Julian Clyne

Mitch Cockman

Helen Coley

Charlotte Cook

Hannah Costigan

Paul Curry

Cyberdyne Systems
    Model 101

Kimberley Dadds

Katy Dale

Gill Darling

Sarah Darmody

Jasmine Davis

Nat Dawson

Marilyn Day

Ellie Dennis

MJ Dias

Ben Donkor

Tim Downie

Maeve Duggan

Rebecca Dunne

Michael 'Bear' East

Lauren Ebersol

Robin Edds

Chris Erikson Jr

Chloe Esposito

Aron Estaver

Anna Everette

Jen Farrant

Emmy Favilla

Alice Feeney

Issy Festing

Jamie Fewery

Cara Fielder

Molly Flatt

Anna Frame

Giles Fraser

Naomi Frisby

Yvette G

Laura Gallant

Jessica Gallop

Maria Ghibu

Janine Gibson

Jennifer Gibson

Angela Giles

Carolyn Gillis

Claire Goodswen

Cyril Goodswen

Gill Goodswen

Richard Goodswen

Rob Goodswen

Josh Goodswen

Daniel Grant

Samantha Grant

Andrew Green

Luke Green

Charlotte Griffiths

Demelza Griffiths

Mike Griffiths

Steve Grimwood

Alessandra Gritt

Karen Hamilton

Dan Hanks

Cleo Harrington

Sam Haysom

Linda Heald

Patricia Healey

Stuart Heritage

Carmen Hernandez

Chris Heywood

Juliette Hill

Lara Hill

Peter Hirst

Jo Hoare

Paul Hood

Dawn Horton

Julie Houston

Karolyn Hubbard

Liam Hudson

Laura Jacoby

Hugh Japeen

Isaac Jay

David Jennings

Helen Jennings

Jamie Jones

Nicola Jones

Kate Kamenitsky

Lizzie Kaye

Jack and Queenie
    Kennedy

Michael Kennedy
Terry Kennedy &
   Caroline Heal
Amy Kensett
Simon Kerr
Dan Kieran
Matt King
Sophie Kipner
Suz Koch
Mackenzie Kruvant
Jean Laight
Ali Land
Adele Lawson
Geoff Leeson
Jessica Leitch
Patrick Lenton
Lucy Lev
Rory Lewarne
Luke Lewis
Richard Lewis
Amy Lord
Charlotte Mac
Sue Machin
Louise Macqueron
Alison Marlow
Elizabeth Masters
Matthew Maytum
Judith McCarter
Lindsay McDowall
Stuart McPhee
Kate McQuaid
Hilary Mitchell
John Mitchinson

Rebecca Mogridge
Des Mohan
Cal Moriarty
Joel Naoum
Carlo Navato
Lindsey Novak
Eva Ntoumou
Carolyn O'Brien
Shane O'Neill
Georgina O'Sullivan
Kelly Oakes
Sarah Patmore
Katy Pegg-Hargreaves
Imogen Pelham
Neely Pessin
Dan Peters
Tom Phillips
Arianna Pipicelli
Chelsey Pippin
Justin Pollard
Max Porter
Nina Pottell
Alex Preston
Kate Price
Marc Price
James Reid
Holly Richardson
Amy Roberts
Emily Roberts
Howard Roberts
Jane Roberts
Margaret Rogers
Daniel Ross

Justin Ross
Lydia Ruffles
William Rycroft
Trisha Sakhlecha
Amna Saleem
Lucy Scholes
Kylie Scott
Alexander Seibt
Mike Shanahan
Nikesh Shukla
Laura Silver
Catherine Sinfield
Leilah Skelton
Richard Skinner
Cynda Sloan
Daniel Smith
Martin Smith
Patrick Smith
Sarah Smith
Jennifer Speight
Margaret Spriggs
Michael Spriggs
Ron Spriggs
Jon Stone
G Leigh Thorpe
Karin Tong
Helen Trevorrow
Primrose Tricker-
   O'Dell
John Tyas
Emma Unsworth
Cara Usher
Anna Valdinger

Louis van Kleeff
Kate Vick
Ben Virdee-Chapman
David Wagner
Maureen &
   Graham Walker
Rafaella Wallace
KeithElena Wallis
Julian Ward
Ryan Ward
Ruth Weaver

Sarah Webster
Ken Whalen
Chris Whitaker
Holly Wildman
Ben Wilkinson
Susan Wilkinson
PJ Willett
Laura Williams
Nat Williams
David Willsdon
Fiona Wilson

Joshua Winning
Don Wood
Katie Khan Wood
Michael Woodson
Ellie Woodward
Gemma Wrigley
Felicia Yap
Theo Yiannaki
Jaime Young